A YOUNG LAWYER'S STORY

JOHN ELLSWORTH

SUBJUDICA PRESS

A YOUNG LAWYER'S STORY

1

The résumé was the $39.99 version without Goals and Hobbies.

"He has no goals," said the Assistant U.S. Attorney.

"He has no hobbies, either," said the Chief of Staff.

They looked down and resumed reading.

The U.S. Attorney's office was hiring in D.C., except the job wasn't advertised, there was only one applicant and the job description wasn't published anywhere. The applicant had only found out about the opening when an FBI agent knocked on the door of the dingy apartment he shared with three law students and invited him into the hallway.

"You're Thaddeus Murfee?" The agent flashed his badge in one smooth motion.

The new law grad's knees buckled and his breath caught in his throat. He could feel his face suddenly go hot and his eye-blink rate double. Nobody ever wanted the FBI to come to the door, especially not when you were smoking pot while studying for the bar exam every night.

"Yes," said Thaddeus. "I'm Thaddeus Murfee. Am I in trouble?"

"The U.S. Attorney wants your résumé. Can you have it ready in an hour?"

Thaddeus Murfee looked puzzled. "Who are you? Are you with the U.S. Attorney?"

At that point, the agent badged the young lawyer a second time, just in case he had missed the first. "FBI. I'm here on a mission from the U.S. Attorney."

The young lawyer's eyes narrowed. His mind raced back over his class in criminal procedure. "Am I in trouble?" He knew there had been too much pot smoking last night. It had grown loud and some classmates--girls--had dropped by. The last music finally went silent just before sunrise.

The FBI agent frowned. "You're not in trouble. At least not that I know of."

"Then why--"

"Your availability for an interview came to our attention."

"Oh." He didn't ask how. You didn't ask the FBI questions. Not when you had just turned twenty-three, had no contacts in the legal community, and were behind on your rent and resorting to pot to calm your bar exam nerves.

"Georgetown Law's employment office gave us your name."

"Why would they do that?"

"Because you graduated third in your class and One and

Two have already accepted offers."

"Oh. I was number three? *Really*?" He had only just graduated. Class standings weren't even posted last time he looked.

"Number three. So what do you say? Can you have a résumé for me in one hour?"

"I guess so. Yes. Do you want to come in?" He hoped not. The place reeked of marijuana and unwashed gym socks. Not your best entree into the world of government law.

"I'm going to hit Benjy's Diner down the street. I'll be back at half-past-two."

"It will be waiting."

The young man extended his hand to shake, but the agent had already turned away and was leaving. The deal had been struck, his backside said; they would meet again, soon.

Three days later, Thaddeus went to the interview as directed. Not as invited, as *directed*, by the same FBI agent.

The meeting was held in secret that mid-May afternoon at the Attorney General's office in Washington, D.C. Thaddeus had been warned not to mention it to anyone, not even to Bud Evans, the owner of the suit he was wearing. The receptionist offered water and coffee; Thaddeus declined. His hands were shaking so bad he was afraid he might slop any liquid down the front of his white shirt. So he waited.

On the other side of the door, three people were meeting. They were an Assistant U.S. Attorney, a chief of staff, and an FBI agent. They had all just finished up with the applicant's dossier, provided by the FBI.

"Well," said the Assistant U.S. Attorney, Melissa McGrant. "He's a kid from a broken home. Family scattered to hell and back. So there's no one around to keep track of him."

All heads nodded. It was good, good that he was alone in the world.

"He's totally broke. Two hundred bucks to his name," said Harold Stuttermeyer, Chief of Staff of the U.S. Attorney's office. Which means he's desperate. We could set him up in a broom closet with a forty-watt bulb and he'd be happy."

"His girlfriend just moved to L.A.," said Naomi Ranski, the FBI agent. "He's lonely and feeling abandoned. He needs to belong somewhere. This is a good time to nab him."

They resumed flipping through the dossier. Naomi Ranski sat idly by, flipping pages without reading; she had put it together. She had also put together the psychological profile, based on surveillance of the new grad and based on his student records at Georgetown Law. He was very introverted with average social skills as he'd never learned how to interact with people of varied social status as most kids would learn by growing up in families. The broken home had definitely stunted his development, said the report. So had the foster homes in his early teens. He was perfect; the Agency preferred introverts with underdeveloped social skills for the kind of job it had in mind for the young applicant. They weren't losers, these kids, not exactly, but they weren't going to turn out to be giants of industry, either.

So far, he was a fit. Now to find out if he could walk and chew gum.

The applicant was brought into the room. No one smiled at him and only McGrant looked up.

Assistant U.S. Attorney McGrant was a New Yorker with a take-no-prisoners approach to handling the government's legal business. She worked the counter-espionage side of the street. She was firm and she was cagey and she never forgot or allowed those around her to forget that they were sworn to defend the laws of the United States and to uphold the U.S. Constitution regardless of the cost. She would be the first to pull the trigger on an enforcement action and the last to leave the courtroom when the prosecution was concluded.

She was in charge of the meeting and no one doubted it. She told Thaddeus to take a seat.

He sat down as ordered and clasped his hands on the table. Then he looked up.

To his right was Harold Stuttermeyer, Chief of Staff for the U.S. Attorney. Stuttermeyer was a fifteen-year lifer on the U.S. Attorney's staff, a man more suited for administrative matters than the trial of criminal cases before juries. McGrant explained that Stuttermeyer sat at the U.S. Attorney's right hand and knew everything about everyone in the office. He had his methods: particularly cyber-surveillance and telephone taps. Thaddeus made a mental note to avoid the guy at all costs should he somehow get hired.

Naomi Ranski was seated directly across the table from the applicant. Ranski was African-American and was heavily muscled across her shoulders and upper arms. She was FBI, but not the same FBI who three times had appeared at the young lawyer's door. She had served on the team that outwitted and arrested Robert Hanssen, the most devious CIA double-agent who had ever betrayed the United States in its entire history. Hansen was currently serving fifteen consecutive life terms at ADX Florence, the federal government's supermax prison at Florence, Colorado. It was rumored Agent Ranski visited Hanssen twice a year, following up on anything new he might be willing to reveal about his spying that could help undo the blows he had dealt his country.

"We're glad you could meet with us," McGrant said to the applicant.

"Do you know why you're here?" asked Stuttermeyer.

FBI agent Ranski answered for Thaddeus. "He only knows that he was selected for the interview based on his class standing. He also knows the job wasn't posted on Georgetown's Law Jobs Board but he's okay with that."

"You know I'm okay with it? Really?" asked Thaddeus. He was surprised at her answer, her claim to know he was okay with the secrecy surrounding the job.

Ranski gave the young lawyer a hard look, a look that telegraphed that she had the goods on him. "Our job is to know where you're going before you even climbs on your Vespa. Our job is to know who's calling before your prepaid cell rings. Our job is to know where you'll bed down even before some lucky girl accepts your offer of a Dutch date. And we're damn good at our job."

"What about you, Stutters?" said McGrant. "Can you sell him to Broyles as a new hire now that you've seen him?"

"I can sell him," said Stuttermeyer. "He'll clean up well and look just like one of us. Speaking of, Mr. Murfee, lose the ponytail. Federal judges don't do ponytails."

They all looked at Thaddeus. The ponytail's time had

passed. He was wearing a troubled navy suit. The coat was a full shade darker than the pants. The sleeves were far too short. Even worse, the pants were a full inch-and-a-half short which, with the coat, left him looking like a desperate scarecrow.

Then, "Mr. Murfee, I'm Assistant U.S. Attorney Melissa McGrant, the gentleman on my left is Harold Stuttermeyer of the U.S. Attorney's office, and this lady across from you is Naomi Ranski, Special Agent, FBI."

A puzzled look crept across Thaddeus' face.

"Forgive me, but FBI? Am I being investigated just for an interview?"

McGrant smiled and shook her head. "We asked you here to talk about the U.S. Attorney's office and an opening."

His puzzlement deepened so he continued, heeding roommate Bud Evans' instructions to him to be pushy and let them know he meant business. "It's a job as a lawyer in the U.S. Attorney's office, right?"

"Yes," said Stuttermeyer, "you would be part of my staff in the U.S. Attorney's office.

"And what part is that?" Thaddeus asked. "Criminal or civil?"

"I'm administrative," Stuttermeyer said, leaning in and speaking conspiratorially, which, to Thaddeus, sounded odd since "administrative" and "conspiratorial" didn't much hang together.

"Would I be going to court?"

"Eventually. But at first your duties would be the common first-year duties: research, writing, liaison with the FBI and

U.S. Marshals, trial preparation. Even the chance to second-chair some motions and evidentiary hearings. That would be about a third of your hours. The other two-thirds would be administrative. You'll get the full run-down your first day."

"But I wouldn't have my own file assignments?"

"Not initially. But that would come. Assuming you stayed on beyond the probationary period, of course."

He narrowed his eyes at Stuttermeyer. "Why wouldn't I?"

Stuttermeyer leaned back in the luxurious green leather chair.

“Sometimes public service isn't a fit for some people. We all have to find our own niche."

"All right. What about salary and benefits? I have to ask. I've been starving for three years." He held up both arms. "Even this suit is borrowed because I can't afford one of my own." Thaddeus sat back and waited. He was grateful that Bud Evans had told him to get right down to the question of salary. "Nothing else matters," Bud had said. "We need income around here before the sheriff starts putting our stuff out on the street."

"Law school must have been very difficult," McGrant said softly. "I'm sorry it's been so hard for you."

He shook his head. "I'm not after sympathy, Ms. McGrant. I only brought it up because I need to start right away in order to keep from getting evicted."

"Would Monday be soon enough?" asked Stuttermeyer.

Thaddeus' jaw fell open. "Yes. I mean, *yes*!"

"So you accept?"

"I accept? Hell yes!"

"Payday two weeks later. And I'll make sure you have enough cash to last until then if I have to float you a loan myself."

"Oh, no, no, I'm not after a handout," Thaddeus said. "But thanks. I have just enough to make it two weeks. But then I'm on the street."

Stuttermeyer held up a hand. "No need for that. Come in Monday at eight sharp and we'll get you right over to HR."

"I accept," Thaddeus said eagerly. "I need this."

"I'll need to spend about an hour with you after we're done here," said Agent Ranski. "Fingerprints, background, mug shot--all the usual stuff. Let's get it out of the way so you can hit the ground running on Monday."

"Whatever you need," Thaddeus agreed. "I'm all yours."

"Wait," said Assistant U.S. Attorney McGrant. "Aren't you forgetting something?"

Stuttermeyer spoke up. "One-hundred-forty-five thousand per annum. With all federal benefits."

The air caught in Thaddeus' throat and he coughed.

"Excuse me. I'm making one-forty-five starting Monday?"

"Yes," said Stuttermeyer. "I'm sorry we can't go any higher."

"No--I can get my own place if I want."

"Yes. Georgetown is expensive, but there are areas farther out."

"Thank you," Thaddeus said. "Thank you so much. I won't let you down. You have my word."

"We know that," said McGrant. "We knew we could count on you."

A look passed between Ranski and McGrant. They had known all along he was down to his last two hundred dollars in student loan money. They had it all: bank balances, names of friends, favorite eateries, favorite beer, records from the foster homes where he'd spent his youth.

He didn't press them any further about the exact nature of his duties. He couldn't; he was too far into picking out furniture for his new apartment. New clothes to wear to work. Maybe a car, as he didn't own one. Selling the used Vespa scooter to some naive freshman.

It was only on the way home on the bus that he realized he hadn't asked them diddly-squat about the job. Only how much and what department. Who would he be reporting to? What kind of insurance would he receive? What about opportunities for advancement?

He hadn't asked and they hadn't offered.

But he was sure it would all work out. After all, it was a government job. The only thing he knew about the government at that point was that it handed out drivers' licenses and paid him survivor's benefits because his parents were dead. It never occurred to him that having no family was part of the non-existent job description.

No one would know anything about him and he still knew zip about them.

Which was exactly how his government wanted it.

2

A roommate named Winnie cut his hair. The cut cost ten bucks plus Thaddeus did the dishes all weekend.

She took off the ponytail with a momentous snip of the scissors. She held it up for Thaddeus to view. He only shrugged. "Keep going," he said.

Thirty minutes later he was in style. In style in a city where one out of every twelve residents was a lawyer and everyone looked the same, from the Brooks Brothers suits to the tassel loafers. Washington, D.C. For three years he had survived there while in law school. Now he was joining the ranks of the employed who served at the altar of the government.

His roommates and friends took up a collection. He rode his Vespa to Men's Warehouse. The suit cost $111 but the store threw in another suit and a sport coat free. The sport coat was a mix and match with both suit pants. Two white shirts were $42 and a blue tie and a red tie were thrown in free.

Next, the roomies handled his transportation needs. A two-week Metro Blue Line pass from Alexandria to D.C. ran him

$33.33. Which left him with a hundred and fifty dollars to last two weeks. It was cutting it close, but he knew he could sneak away at lunch and grab a three-dollar meal at Burger King--a law school standby.

Then it was Monday morning and everyone had an opinion about which suit with which tie. In the end, Bud Evans contributed his favorite Club Tie to the mix and Thaddeus headed out for the bus stop. "You're the real deal, Murf," Bud told him. "Now don't take any shit off anybody."

By 7:45 a.m. he arrived at 4th Street NW and ten minutes later was waiting in the U.S. Attorney's reception area for Mr. Stuttermeyer. He was still waiting at eight-thirty when the woman who had interviewed him swept into reception and led him away down a long hall to a dark conference room. She switched on the light and took the chair on the far side of the small table. At the hiring meeting last week Melissa McGrant had smiled every now and then; this morning she wasn't smiling at all--not even once. She motioned for him to shut the door and he closed it behind him and took the seat across from her. He studied her as she opened a folder, probably his employee file, he guessed. She read for several moments and he watched. He knew her name was Melissa McGrant. She was tall, a woman who favored necklace pendants that lay in the hollow of her throat, and tiny diamond earrings, barely more than chips. She wore very little makeup around her violet eyes and just a hint of blush above ruby lip gloss that emphasized her perfect bow of a mouth. Anymore than that about her was pure guesswork.

"Morning, Thaddeus. Let me tell you a little bit about why you're here."

"Excuse me, but I thought I was meeting with Mr. Stuttermeyer. He said I would be answering to him." Three people had interviewed him: McGrant, Stuttermeyer and the FBI agent, Ranski.

She shook her head. "You'll be answering to *me* while you're working here. You were told to come in and ask for Mr. Stuttermeyer today because that's the way it would normally happen. But normal isn't you."

Thaddeus was perplexed. He had been told he was answering to Stuttermeyer, the Chief of Staff of the U.S. Attorney's office.

"So I'm working for you?"

"Long story short: you're working for Mr. Stuttermeyer but you answer to me. We good?"

"We're good."

He started to make a note in his notebook but she reached across the narrow table and put her hand on his.

"Please. Don't write any of this down when you and I meet or talk by phone. No notes--ever."

"Understand. No notes."

"Now, let me tell you a little about the office. The United States Attorney's Office for the District of Columbia is unique among U.S. Attorney's Offices in the scope of its work. It serves as both the local and the federal prosecutor for the nation's capital. On the local side, we have prosecutions for everything from misdemeanor drug possession cases to murders. On the federal side, we have everything from child pornography to gangs and financial fraud to terrorism."

"So where do I fit in?"

She stood up and went to the door. Opening it just a crack, she peered out and looked up and down the hallway. She closed it again and sat down. "This room was swept just twenty minutes ago. We should be good."

Thaddeus looked around the tiny room. Swept? For bugs?

She continued. "Like I said, you will answer to me. But you will assist the U.S. Attorney, Franklin J. Broyles. You will sit outside the door to his office and run his daily calendar. You will observe him and report to me."

"Report what to you?"

"Everything. When he gets to work, what time he leaves. Who calls, who comes in. What he had for lunch, what color his tie was. Everything."

"Why would you want to know those things? I thought I was hired as a lawyer."

"We need to know those things because some questions have come up about Mr. Broyles."

"What kind of questions?"

"Not important. For now, you're my eyes and ears in his office. That's all I can tell you, Mr. Murfee."

"I thought I was another lawyer here."

"You'll be functioning as the U.S. Attorney's administrative aide in almost all respects. But the title is Appointments Secretary."

"So I'm a secretary and I answer to you. Doesn't that make me a spy?"

"That is *exactly* what you are." She leaned across the narrow table, placing her face ten inches away. She whispered, "You will spy on U.S. Attorney Broyles and report back everything about him to me. We have questions about him. That's all I can tell you right now."

"But I came here to practice law."

"If you're successful in this assignment you'll be able to name any job in the federal government you like, and we'll put you there with a huge promotion. We can also get you into any private law firm you might like to work for instead. Or we can get you into the FBI or CIA or NSA. We can also help you with a commission in the military as a JAG officer. Your choice, Thaddeus. Your reward for a job well done. Oh, and there's also a bonus."

"Bonus? For what?"

"Under the Secrecy Act the government pays a five-hundred-thousand-dollar bonus to any employee who helps convict a traitor."

Thaddeus was jolted. A traitor? It rattled him. He struggled to think it through. It wasn't anything he even wanted to touch, ratting on someone. Still, five hundred thousand dollars would be a life-changing event. Plus, they could get him on with the biggest law firm in the country.

"I'm not so sure. I need time to think."

"Well, it's too late now. You've already accepted the job and I've also given you classified information. You can't just walk away."

He straightened up in his chair. "Hold on. What if I did? What's to stop me?"

She scowled at him. "Really? You'd never work as a lawyer, for starters. We'd make sure of that. We would blackball you with every bar association in the U.S. We would warn all employers away from you. We would make your life hell. So don't piss me off. We could also prosecute you."

"*Pros*ecute me? What the hell for?"

"Oh, you needn't worry about that. We'd think of something. You're on our team now and there you'll stay until we're done."

The frustration shot through him like a bolt. He could always find a different job. Or could he?

"I want out."

"Too late. You accepted the position."

"Prove it."

She frowned and laughed without smiling. "What, you don't think we were recording you at your interview last week? I think your exact words were 'I accept? Hell yes!'"

"I remember saying that. You didn't tell me you were recording me."

"So sue us. Are you ready to get to work now?"

The color had drained from his face. His hands looked translucent and weak in the pale room light.

He had been had.

"Do I have any choice?"

"Your choices all went away the day you graduated third in your class."

"I worked hard for that."

"You should be proud. Tell you what."

She pulled open her shoulder bag and produced a twenty-dollar bill.

"Here's twenty bucks. Buy your friends the first round. On me."

"I don't need your damn money."

"Yes, you do. After buying all of your clothes this weekend you're almost broke. Take the twenty, buy a round, and tell them what a bitch I am. Only don't tell them my name. That *is* something you could be prosecuted for."

Thaddeus drew a deep breath and reached to the table.

The twenty-dollar bill was inside his pocket when she showed him to Stuttermeyer's office to be sworn in and introduced around to everyone.

When he turned at the door to tell her goodbye, she was gone.

"Thaddeus!" Stuttermeyer called to him. Still reeling, Thaddeus blinked and stepped inside. The man's desk featured two banker's lamps and a moribund plant.

"Mr. Stuttermeyer," Thaddeus said. They shook hands ferociously.

"Ready to hit the ground running?"

For just a moment he couldn't come up with a reply. Words

escaped him.

Then he managed, "Yes."

Stuttermeyer waved him over to his desk. Thaddeus knew a little about him from his hiring interview. The man was a lifer on the U.S. Attorney's staff, someone more suited for administrative matters than the trial of criminal cases before juries.

"So. You met with Ms. McGrant?"

"Just now."

"What did she have to say?"

"She told me to keep my mouth shut."

"Attaboy. She's big on keeping secrets."

Which was when Thaddeus surrendered. They had him. He had read spy novels about this kind of thing. There was only one thing to do.

He drew a deep breath, blinked hard, and leaned up to the desk.

"Where's my office, Mr. Stuttermeyer? I want to get the hell to work."

3

Stuttermeyer led him to Franklin J. Broyles' office, where he would be working. It took up the front corner of the building; the FBI building was just across the street. The waiting area, where Thaddeus' desk was located, was overrun by blue leather and solid mahogany.

"They sweep every half hour. You'll get used to it and won't even notice."

I won't notice anyway, thought Thaddeus. *I'll be too busy watching Mr. Broyles and reporting on his shoe style and necktie pattern.*

"You'll sit at this desk and greet the visitors when they come in. You'll take their names and let the U.S. Attorney know they're here. You'll offer them something to drink and then go back to whatever. Don't question them. Most people coming to your office will be undercover cops or FBI who really won't want to self-reveal. So leave them to themselves."

"That won't be hard," Thaddeus said. "But it sounds like I'm a waiter. No beef with waiters, but I went to college for seven years to serve coffee?"

"Don't be upset about that. It's really a chance for you to interact with the law enforcement you'll be dealing with when you get your own caseload. It's a good thing for your career. Several of our key trial lawyers have begun their careers right where you'll be sitting."

Thaddeus frowned. He knew he was stuck. But he couldn't resist: "Serving drinks is good for my career? Sounds like HR is staffed by chimpanzees."

Stuttermeyer ignored him, having already moved on to getting Thaddeus set up. He was seated at Thaddeus' desk, entering passwords on the computer and checking the young lawyer's network access.

"Okay, look over my shoulder. This folder here is your access to all files being prosecuted by this office. These files are top secret. Now you know why the FBI did a background check and you've been given a provisional security clearance. This button over here brings up the security camera views inside and outside the office. This link here is for legal research."

"I'll be doing some research? Maybe working on some cases?"

"Not at first. You'll be running errands for the U.S. Attorney and keeping his calendar along with the visitors and drink orders."

"What kind of errands?"

"You know, pick up dry cleaning, grab a kid from kindergarten and run them home, shop for the wife's anniversary present. The usual stuff new lawyers do in the office."

"Ehhh!" Thaddeus made the sound of a buzzer eliminating a game show contestant. "New lawyers don't haul kids around and serve coffee to visitors. New lawyers litigate."

"Why worry? The pay's the same whether you're litigating or chasing down dry cleaning. Plus, there's the status of telling Georgetown fillies that you work for the U.S. Attorney. Not many lawyers have that honor in this town though thousands of them wish they did."

Thaddeus sighed. Stuttermeyer was right about the pay. It was very attractive when you were broke and the sheriff was coming to put your bed out on the sidewalk.

"All right, let me try the desk, please."

AN HOUR LATER, while Thaddeus was randomly clicking Facebook links, the U.S. Attorney, Franklin J. Broyles, came quietly into the office. He was carrying two bulging briefcases and was surrounded by serious men wearing frowns. As they approached, Thaddeus could clearly make out the holsters concealed under their coats. Broyles didn't even so much as look at him as they passed by and disappeared into Broyles' office. The door closed behind them. It wasn't a full minute later before the door re-opened and Broyles came back out, alone this time. He closed the door behind him.

"You're Thaddeus. My new assistant." He was smiling and immediately stuck out his hand. He was warm and welcoming as they passed introductions back and forth.

"I'm an easy guy to work for, Thaddeus. I've already read your résumé and know a little about you and I'm impressed.

We'll get along very well. Now, Jeannette and I would like to have you over for dinner Saturday and get to know everyone better. Can you make it? Bring a date?"

Thaddeus smiled. The man was engaging and was inviting him to his home. The young lawyer was having second thoughts about spying on the guy.

"Sure, I'd like to come. I don't have a date."

"That's fine. Nikki is home for the weekend. She's a student at Harvard. We'll let you two get to know each other and you won't be lonely for someone your own age to shoot the breeze with. Plus I imagine there's lots you can tell her about law school. Number three in your class? I'm very impressed. I was about halfway down my own class roster. I have this job today not because I'm a top student but because I'm a political animal. Always remember, Thad, it isn't what you know, it's who you know. Anyway, I'll tell Nikki you're coming. She's pre-law and will get a kick out of picking your brain. We'll be casual, no ties or coats, so be prepared to have a great dinner, a little wine, and some good talk. We'll firm up later this week."

"I--I--"

"Good. Then put it on my calendar," Broyles said with a laugh. He tossed off a salute and passed back into his own office. "Catch you later," he said.

Thaddeus was at once relieved and impressed. This was already shaping up as not so bad. And there was a daughter? Three years younger and Harvard? He should be so lucky.

For the next few hours he investigated the computer network, found where he had access and where he didn't, and was wondering whether they were tracking him. That's random, he thought; of course they are. Then Broyles suddenly buzzed him on the intercom.

"Let's grab lunch. I've got some agents with me I'd like you to meet. We good?"

"Good," Thaddeus said. He hung up. Dinner Saturday? Lunch today? What wasn't to like?

He clicked on the appointments calendar. It was time to make two entries.

Each one would have his name on it.

Major score. Wait until he told Winnie and Bud back home. This thing might just really work out. The first day couldn't be going any better. The last thing he felt like was a spy.

Broyles impressed Thaddeus again before lunch. He handed Thaddeus a check for five thousand dollars. It was drawn on the U.S. Attorney's general account.

"Buy a couple of new suits," Broyles told him. "Lose the Men's Warehouse look. You're in the big leagues now, Thaddeus, and I need you to look the part."

"I'll pay you back on payday."

"No need. Your government pays for everything we do. Speaking of, let's get lunch. Do you like French?"

FOR LUNCH they gathered at Le B Bistro, a small French place on, of course, B Street.

Thaddeus admired the restaurant, taking it all in before

they sat. It was Broyles, Thaddeus, and the same two severe looking FBI agents. Coffee was ordered all around. Someone mentioned the NFL. For the next five minutes, talk revolved around the Redskins, then the Wizards, and then drifted off into a general rehash of cases filed by the office. The agents served as part of the FBI's counter-terrorism task force. Thaddeus was elated. What could only be described as confidential information was openly discussed in front of him. Voices were kept low but the diners around them seemed totally disinterested anyway. He reminded himself to take mental notes of the discussions so he could report back to Ms. McGrant. But then he told himself no, he liked Mr. Broyles too much to spy on him. He decided on a compromise: he would tell her about the Redskins and the Wizards but wouldn't tell her about the investigations they discussed. That should keep her happy.

After lunch, Broyles dropped Thaddeus at the office and then left for a meeting that appeared nowhere on his calendar. The U.S. Attorney was very close-mouthed. He said nothing about where he was going and Thaddeus didn't ask. Thaddeus took the elevator upstairs and returned to his desk.

Fifteen minutes later, Melissa McGrant walked in.

"Thaddeus," she said grimly, "we need to talk. Let's take a walk."

They went downstairs and stepped out onto 4th Street, where they headed north to F Street and strolled down to the National Building Museum. They entered and took a bench in the midst of the various porticoes, where they could talk.

"You're in place, and that's good," said McGrant. "You had lunch with Broyles and two agents. You enjoyed your Alfredo with linguini. That's good. So here's what I'm looking for. I need you to go into Mr. Broyles' office while he's not there and try to access his briefcase."

She held up a tiny silver item that resembled a hearing aid battery.

"This is a mike. It can hear through briefcases and even drywall. I want you to hide this inside his briefcase. Use your noodle, number three in your class. It's a microphone. It's self-adhering, just peel off this stuff on the back. See here?

Thaddeus looked. He shook his head.

"No," he said.

"No?"

"You want me to violate Mr. Broyles' trust? I have no problem keeping you updated on his calendar, but don't you people have spooks for stuff like this?"

He was put off. He was still feeling defensive about his new friend.

"Yes, we have spooks. And you're one of them. So climb down off your high horse and do the fuck what I'm telling you or we're going to have trouble." Her face turned violet and her voice rose up through clenched teeth. "Mr. Broyles might get his feelings hurt on down the road and that's sad. But you cross me and I'll fucking bury you! Now take the damn mike!"

He gasped in shock. No one had ever spoken to him like

that--at least not since leaving foster care. He succumbed, meekly holding out his hand. She dropped the bug onto his palm.

"If anyone catches you just tell them you need your boss's receipts for his expense account. Understand?"

"Yes. But please, don't ask me to do something like this again."

"Why not? You're a spy now."

He began to respond. It was a moment of cognitive dissonance. On the one hand, they said he was a spy. On the other hand, Broyles made him feel like a family friend. The internal standoff felt like mental handcuffs and he worried that his thinking wasn't reliable just then. He decided he would let Bud in on the secret and get his feedback. Bud would have the right ideas.

She leaned back on the museum bench and smiled the Assistant U.S. Attorney smile she had greeted him with at the interview.

"You'll do just fine. And next time, don't argue with me. You're working for *me*. *Never* forget that. And here's something else. The U.S. Attorney is not your friend. He's a personable man and can be very charming. But he's also selling state secrets, so buck up. You're a key figure in U.S. counterintelligence now. We're all counting on you."

His eyes rolled up and he blurted, "This isn't what I expected at all!"

"Just get this mike hidden, Thaddeus. Don't worry about notifying me. We'll know once it's placed."

Thaddeus looked away. Fighting with his supervisor was nonproductive, especially if what she said about Broyles was true. As he had twice before that day, he let it go. Then he stood up and he heard himself talking.

"Mr. Broyles is gone from the office. Let's go plant a bug."

4

A firm resolve was hard. Thaddeus crept into his office amidst feelings of deepening guilt. He hated what they were asking him to do. He had never been one to go behind anyone's back and trick them. That just wasn't who he was. But it always came back to the same thing: working for the U.S. Attorney was an honor. It was a great job and he didn't want to blow it. But why couldn't he have just been hired on to be a regular attorney? He was beginning to dislike Ms. McGrant in a big way. He was being used. He decided it couldn't wait until that night. He called Bud Evans and got through on the third beep of the cell phone.

"Bud, Thaddeus."

"Hey, Thad."

"Weird things going on around here, Bud."

"Wait," said Bud. "You're at the U.S. Attorney's Office, Thad? All right, just assume the phone we're talking on is bugged. Whatever you need to say, let's wait until tonight. Anything else I can help you with?"

Clearly Bud was withholding. Thaddeus couldn't blame the guy. He had a future to worry about too.

"Listen, would you call me in about four minutes? On my cell phone? I might say something odd back to you, but just stay on the phone. Would you do that?"

"Yes. What's it about?"

"Just do it, Bud. I'll explain it all when I get home tonight."

"Okay, Thaddeus."

He hung up and replaced the handset in its cradle on the desk.

Then he approached the door to his boss's office. It was closed. He started to try the knob but pulled back. Actually, Thaddeus had been gone with Ms. McGrant and he couldn't say for absolutely certain that his boss hadn't returned; he could only guess. So he put his ear up to the door and listened. Nothing. He hurried back to his desk and hit the intercom to Broyles' office. He waited and waited but there was no answer. Only then did he make his decision.

Returning to the closed door, he twisted the knob and pushed into the office where his boss might be lurking.

But he wasn't. Thaddeus hastened across the carpet to Broyles' desk. There was no briefcase in or around the desk. So he crouched down and investigated beneath.

Bingo.

The briefcase was leather, black, with embossed initials just below the handles: FJB.

He grasped the handles and gently lifted it out from under

the desk. He worked the button beneath the handle. It was unlocked, so he opened the case and peered inside. It was empty. He felt around the inner lip of the briefcase for an opening where he could insert the microphone.

Halfway around the inside with his fingers, Thaddeus heard voices out in his own office. The door was still open between the two and he realized with a bolt of fear that the voices were coming closer. They were coming toward Broyles' office.

He quickly stood and pushed the case back under the desk with his foot. His leg was still outstretched when a four-wheeled cart rolled into the office.

Then his phone chimed.

"This is Thaddeus."

He paused.

"Yes, Mr. Broyles, I'm looking for it right now. Are you sure you didn't take it with you?"

Then he hung up.

Frank: it was the custodian who came through twice a day and carted away papers for shredding. He was accompanied by a young man dressed similarly. Both men stopped, and Frank's eyes narrowed.

"You in Mr. Broyles' office," he said.

"It's all right," Thaddeus replied. "That was him on the phone."

"Mr. Broyles, he said no one's to come into his office but me. That's all."

"Well, he didn't tell me that. I'm actually looking for receipts for his expense account."

"Well, mister," said Frank, "you might and you might not be doing all that. All's I know is you ain't supposed to be in here. Now look here, sir. I ain't got nothing against you and you're probably only doing your job. But I'm gonna have to tell Mr. Broyles you was in here. That's *my* job."

Thaddeus backed away from Broyles' desk and held up his hands.

"Look, I don't have anything that belongs to Mr. Broyles. Now you can tell him all you want to tell him or you can forget. I hope you'll forget because sometime you might need me to cut you some slack. Are you with me, Frank?"

Frank's face drew up in a scowl. He was older, maybe early sixties. His face said he rejected any and all bullshit.

"We agree," Frank said. "But on one condition. I ever catch you in here again, I'm telling. Ambrose is standing right here. He can back me up. But for now, Ambrose," he said, turning to his assistant, "we gonna agree to let it go. Nobody saw nothing here today. We all good?"

"I ain't seen shit," said Ambrose. "Don't even care about none of it."

"And I'm good," said Thaddeus.

"Me, too," said Frank. "Something else for you to know. Mr. Broyles' office is shielded. Ain't no cell phone reception in here. You must be new. We done now."

Thaddeus circled around the men and hurried back into his office, where he dropped down into his chair and exhaled a long sigh. That had been close. So close. And now someone was onto him. Someone who was evidently loyal to Mr. Broyles. Thaddeus shook his head. Frank might still go to Broyles; he would never be sure. But it was the best he could do. He had tried to short-circuit the tattletale. He prayed he had.

Then he opened his left fist. As he did so, he remembered. The microphone. He had been palming the microphone. But when his hand opened he saw, to his horror, the microphone was no longer there. His heart jumped in his chest. Jesus, had he dropped the damn thing inside the briefcase? Or on the floor?

Just then, Mr. Broyles opened the hallway door and came striding inside. This time he was alone and he had a pained look on his face. He came directly toward Thaddeus.

"I've been hearing things about you, Mr. Murfee," he said as he approached.

"What--what--" Thaddeus managed to mutter.

"I've been hearing they only offered you the minimum starting salary. I fixed that and you're now at one-seventy-five a year. This is cause for celebration. Saturday night we'll open a bottle of bubbly and make some toasts."

"That sounds great, sir. I'd like that."

"Oh, and one other thing. I talked to Nikki. She says she's excited to meet you."

"Oh, that's good news. I'm sure we'll be good friends."

"I'm sure you will."

"Okay."

The door closed behind Broyles. Frank and Ambrose emerged a few minutes later. Frank looked at Thaddeus as he pushed the cart past. But he didn't say anything, just gave him a disgusted look.

Alone, Thaddeus tried to calm his shaking hands. He tugged at his collar. He wanted to loosen his tie but the office had a policy against untied ties. So he sat there, numb, eyes shut, trying to calm his racing heart.

Thaddeus could only imagine what Frank said to Broyles.

His thoughts returned to the missing mike, his next big problem.

He wondered if he had left a fingerprint on it. He guessed not, but on the other hand he didn't know what the FBI might be able to get off the mike anyway if it was found. DNA? A partial print? He had no idea.

He decided he wouldn't tell McGrant about losing her bug. He needed at least one full paycheck before he got fired for blowing it so miserably. At least one paycheck, he prayed.

Which he knew was futile. This was the same God who had refused to give him parents during seven years of foster homes.

And now he felt just as vulnerable as he always had.

So he had been wrong. Becoming a lawyer hadn't cured those feelings after all.

They were only worse.

5

Sing Di Hoa stepped off the metro rail in Eastern Beijing at nine a.m. and was immediately struggling for oxygen in an atmosphere of auto exhaust, wood smoke, and dirty coal.

He turned north on Ca Lam Street and began making his way toward the offices of Ministry of State Security--MSS--the Chinese equivalent of the CIA. Today would be a bright day both for the Chinese people and for Hoa personally. He had engaged with a high-ranking American official in Washington D.C. and today would be the day his efforts paid off with a huge data dump consisting of American nuclear policy--America's fall back in case of financial destabilization between China and the United States. A trillion cubic feet of greenback dollars was owed by the U.S. to China in 2010, a tectonic shift if the Asians suddenly decided to declare the money due and owing.

The coveted, classified data told the story of America's response if China suddenly declared all debt obligations due and owing, which it had the right to do at any time, even on a mere whimsy. Such a declaration would catch the Americans with no legitimate economic response. If such a call-up were to occur, the U.S. could only leverage its position with an intense military response that could consist of anything from off-shore war games to actual attacks on the Chinese mainland. It was Sing Di Hoa's task to discover what that response actually would be, and today he had done just that.

February of 2010 ushered in another Year of the Tiger according to the twelve-year cycle of the traditional Chinese lunar calendar. It also marked a time of pre-ordained political change. Over the following year and a half, the leaders of China's Communist Party and civilian government would hand over power to the next generation.

Initially, observers both inside and outside China presumed that the years 2010-2013 would see an orderly transition of power and the untroubled retirement of a generation of party-state leaders, from Communist Party General Secretary Hu Jintao and State Premier Wen Jiabao downwards. Even within China's Communist Party, however, there were already signs of discontent--over corruption, social anomie and the perceived stagnation of the economy and the political system. A Chinese-United States economic meltdown had been made all the more conceivable by this same discontent. The war plans were critical at that point.

Hoa approached the MSS building, a century-old mishmash of concrete and steel that attempted to project a feeling of power but actually projected a failed engineering policy.

He presented security credentials and waited in an impatient line of downstream political workers for the eye scan. Hoa was forty-five, lithe and powerfully built, with a penchant for Western food and Japanese martial arts and a live-in girlfriend--one of the few social accommodations the Party allowed to ease the pain of living in a communist country with such huge economic disparities among its citizens. What might seem a reasonable price for a one-bedroom to a Party official would, in most cases, be unthinkable to a security operative as low in the food chain as Hoa. Consequently, he shared a studio apartment of four hundred square feet with his girlfriend ten miles from city center in a crowded, noisy community of Party worker-bees and Ministry subordinates.

The credentials officer was satisfied at last and waved Hoa on through the wall of scanners and screens. Hoa headed off to the elevator bank and searched for one that wasn't under repair. He was able to crowd onto the second car with a dozen others and stare with them at the flickering floor numbers as they silently rose up to their cubicles.

At his desk he placed his lunch inside the bottom right drawer and settled onto his hard cubicle chair. His eyes immediately focused on his computer screen, on which were the words: Longma Kee 9 a.m.

Hoa checked his watch. Less than five minutes. He'd had no idea the Director wanted to meet with him until that very moment and his pulse raced in anticipation of a meeting with the brains of the MSS. His work had gone well but he didn't realize it had gone *that* well, enough to have captured the attention of the MSS's highest-ranking official.

Hoa headed for the communal restroom where he pushed his way through elbows and shoulders up to the long communal sink with its many spouting water taps. He cupped a teaspoon of water in his hand and patted it on his head, attempting to flatten the challenging cowlick nature had blessed him with. It was no use: the cowlick gave up nothing to the water. He straightened up while being jostled from side to side and studied himself in the stainless steel mirror--a poor excuse for glass but workable and common in all Beijing public restrooms.

Disappointed that his coarse hair had remained uncontrollable again, Hoa departed the restroom and hurried to the elevators, where he ascended another twenty-two floors .

He stepped off and found himself in a rich lobby of muted reds and golds--the official Party colors. He had been up here twice before but never to visit with Director Kee.

He gave one of the six receptionists his name and again produced security credentials and allowed the eye scans that were around every corner in the MSS. The receptionist told him to walk to the open door at the end of the hall behind her, that he was exactly on time and the Director was waiting. Hoa bowed his neck and struck out.

Director Longma Kee was a stout, moribund character straight out of Chinese noir films, a humorless man who didn't smile when Hoa entered his office without knocking. It was rumored his condition was terminal, but that rumor was now at least two years old. He was alone in the huge expanse of office.

Hoa crossed the deep carpet and waited at the four visitors' chairs until the Director looked up from his paperwork and indicated Hoa should take a seat. Hoa sat on cue and placed his hands on his knees.

"We have received and inventoried the drop," the Director said without introduction.

"From Broyles in Washington?"

"Yes. The package consisted of two flash drives. The response plans are included and numbered one to ten, just as promised. The worst case scenario is what we feared: an all-out nuclear attack on our homeland."

Hoa shook his head slowly. The news was so dire that he didn't have the words to respond.

"Well?" said the Director, evidently seeking Hoa's response even though it wasn't his to make.

"I'm shocked but not surprised," Hoa said slowly. "The Americans never cease to amaze with their ardent desire to make war as a financial last stand. They are still taking their battle plans from George Custer, the army officer who was defeated at--"

"--at Little Bighorn. The ill-advised American cavalry officer who failed to assess his enemy's strength and died for it. Do you think that's the situation here?"

"The Americans presently have a fleet of seventy nuclear submarines with nuclear launch capabilities, between the Fast-Attack class and the Boomers. We have three times that. It would be foolish for them to consider striking us. Their cities and infrastructure would be vaporized minutes after."

The Director smiled. He liked Hoa. But he needed more and he wondered whether Hoa was, in fact, the proper asset to pull off what Kee envisioned. Hoa's control had quickly named him for the follow-up; it was up to the Director to decide.

"You have been selected to travel to America and meet with Mr. Broyles. There you will demand the alternative battle plans for such a strike. We believe there will be at least one dozen war games. Broyles will claim he has no access, but you won't be thwarted. He can get what you are demanding and he can make it available to you. You will be provided with passports, money, disguises, new identities and even citizenship credentials as an American citizen. You will obtain all battle plans and make your country proud."

Hoa's heart leapt in his chest. "When am I to do this?"

"Tonight. You will speak with Broyles today and leave for America tonight."

"Director, I--"

"You're the right man to do this, Comrade Hoa. Broyles trusts you and will respond to the American dollars we have wired to your bank account in California."

"Mr. Director, I am stunned. I don't know how to thank you for this honor to serve."

"You have proven your value. You will succeed and return a hero to our people."

"One question, if I may. Why not just penetrate the American server network and steal the war plans?"

"We've tried. We would leave fingerprints."

"You have honored me today, Comrade Director. I will not let you down."

"No, but if you did let me down there would be no country for you to return to," the Director said with an easy smile.

"You would never see your family. So think on this while you leave Hong Kong to fly to San Francisco."

"I will. I will think hard about it."

"Just don't let me down. If you have to die for this, do it on American soil. Not here at home."

6

Sing Di Hoa pulled shut the articulating door of the phone booth. The overhead light blinked but went dark. He lifted the handset and punched in the unfamiliar American area code and seven-digit number. Then he waited as it rang once, twice, three times. "Come on, come on," he whispered into the mouthpiece.

Then, "Frank Broyles. How can I help?"

Hoa placed the voice scrambler against the mouthpiece.

"I'm here," said Hoa. No introduction, no name--nothing to indicate the caller's ID. At Broyles' end, the inbound voice was electronic.

"All the same," said Broyles. Then he added: "All the same, I think you have a wrong number."

Which meant: same time, same day of the week, same location, and same payment as the last meeting. He knew whoever was on the other end of the call would know the particulars.

Broyles hung up.

He walked to the window in his office and looked out at 4th Street NW and there, to the south, his eyes played over the District of Columbia Court of Appeals. He shook his head then reached up and pressed the thumb and middle finger of his right hand softly against his closed eyes. It was a reassuring feeling, a temporary distancing from the world of spies and counterspies that he now inhabited. Inhabited voluntarily from the first moment he agreed to meet with the man claiming to be from the Chinese Embassy when they had bumped into each other at the National Gallery.

He had known it would come sooner or later, the contact by the Chinese; the FBI, during his orientation as the new U.S. Attorney for the District of Columbia, had warned him that U.S. officials were routinely contacted by the Chinese. Those contacted were to inform the FBI so the Chinese agent would be deported back to China as yet another failed spy. It was all routine. The whole world of foreign embassies in D.C. was just one big revolving door with spies coming and going, secrets coming and going, monies coming and going until someone got their name in the paper and was outed, whereupon an example would be made of him when he was sent off to a maximum security prison built into the side of a Colorado mountain. Another warning to others who might consider selling their country's secrets.

Hell, he thought, lifting his eyes and looking further south toward the Superior Court of D.C., everyone who was anyone was selling. Half the Congress, a Supreme Court Justice, four spooks out of the NSA, hundreds of faceless nobodies in the EOB--everyone was on the take in exchange for secrets. Whether selling to the Chinese or the Russkies or the fucking Bangladeshi, U.S. Secrets were being distributed to overseas computers hourly.

But what made Broyles unique--what made his briefcase worth a million dollars--was the war games. The games the U.S. endlessly invented and played against the CIA database so that various scenarios could be studied and embellished according to how sick the U.S. meant to make the enemy with obscene germ warfare, or how extinct the U.S. meant to make the enemy's food supply with plagues of genetically modified insects, or how brightly the people of Beijing or Moscow could be made to glow by a nuclear airburst at ten thousand feet versus twenty thousand feet.

These were the matters being fed by Broyles to Hoa and his predecessors. The data was priceless to the countries at the receiving end of the American war plans. Maybe not priceless, Broyles corrected himself; in fact, there was a price. One million dollars a bag. Sometimes a bag held one plan; sometimes a hundred. He never knew, he never asked, he never cared. Only the deposit advices he received from his off-shore accounts mattered to him. It was all there was for an old man who was said to be sick and dying and needed money to leave his wife and children. That was the official story on Broyles. It's what the Chinese would know about him.

He pulled back from his window and sat at his desk. It was time to call his handlers.

Broyles needed new secrets.

7

The Georgetown Reservoir was part of the water supply and treatment infrastructure for the District of Columbia. It was located in the Palisades neighborhood of Washington, D.C., approximately two miles downstream from the Maryland--D.C. boundary. Broyles and Hoa would meet at the sluice gate just beyond the Army Corp of Engineers castle.

Broyles headed there on his Piaggio three-wheeler, a huge motor scooter that proved its worth when Broyles evaded any FBI tails by filtering through standstill traffic on the freeways he took. While the four-wheelers and eighteen-wheelers were jammed up, Broyles whizzed between them, close enough to the vehicles on either side to reach out and touch them as he sailed past.

At 8:56 he wheeled into the small parking lot at the sluice gate, parked without the need for a kickstand, leapt off, and jogged over to the meet. The DoD briefcase banged against his thigh as he went.

He put his back against the chain link fence protecting the sluice and waited.

Then it was 9:06 and Broyles knew something was wrong. Hoa was late and the Chinese were never late. Not in the half-dozen times they had already met and exchanged. So Broyles casually let himself down onto the grass where he sat cross-legged, the briefcase on the ground in front of him. He closed his eyes and slowly counted. Halfway to one hundred, automobile headlights bounced into the parking lot from beyond and his heart jumped. Was it him? He craned his head around and watched. But the automobile continued rolling, making a complete circle and then leaving the lot and the connecting road just as abruptly as it had arrived.

Broyles was at eighty-seven when he stood.

At one hundred, it was all over. He was jogging again toward the Piaggio, where he threw open the seat lid and fitted the briefcase down into the roomy well below. Slamming the lid shut, he climbed on the bike, keyed it up, and roared out of the lot.

He headed for the Palisades, one of the lesser-known neighborhoods in Washington, consisting of a mixture of detached houses, townhouses and apartments. The homes along the bluff on Potomac Avenue offered a broad view of the Potomac River and the Virginia riverfront as he rode by, continuing his journey back to his Georgetown condo.

The following afternoon, Friday, while Broyles was inside Conference Room III meeting with several assistants, Thaddeus received a call from Hoa. Again, no identification, no name, just an electronic voice instructing Thaddeus to deliver this message to his boss: *All the same, tonight.*

Thaddeus buzzed Reception and told them to take calls. He then crept away to McGrant's office. He was escorted right inside, where he found McGrant sipping a diet drink and dictating into a microphone. She looked up.

"Thaddeus," she said. "You must have news."

"I got a call. Broyles is meeting someone tonight. I have no idea who."

"Follow him."

"Me? Why would I do that? Why not the FBI?"

"Because no one else can know. We aren't sure who we can trust at this point. Just do as I say, Thaddeus, and for God's sake stop questioning me every time I tell you to do something."

"I don't like it. I have no training for this."

"You have no training to follow someone? Actually, it works out perfectly. Broyles lost the man you replaced last month. He did it on a goddamn motor scooter. You've got a motor scooter. You're perfectly suited for this job."

"Wait. You hired me because I ride a Vespa? That was the criteria?"

"Don't be silly. Of course not."

Thaddeus hurried back to his office. Broyles was still in conference. Thaddeus informed Reception he was again taking calls. Had he missed any? The answer was no, he had not. He breathed a sigh of relief and busied himself with his computer while his mind raced ahead.

At six o'clock, Thaddeus drove home and had a beer with Bud Evans. Bud was his roommate of seven years. They had no secrets. Until now. Thaddeus needed to talk to someone, but Bud wasn't the one—not after Thaddeus had begun to understand how much trouble he was in. No, he needed a professional. Who could he turn to for advice about all this? It left him saddened. These were the times a young man needed a father. He had been deprived of that and had made enough wrong turns in his life to deeply regret it. So he smiled superficially at Bud, shared a laugh, and mentally prepared for what lay ahead.

At 8:50 p.m., Broyles was followed by Thaddeus as he roared up MacArthur Boulevard. Thaddeus was riding two cars behind on his cream Vespa scooter. Then there was a freeway maneuver intended to lose any tailing vehicles where Broyles threw caution to the wind and suddenly cut back across the median and proceeded back to the next connecting street then again turned onto MacArthur Boulevard. Thaddeus followed. Broyles went through a late yellow light, roared up five blocks, and veered off through the Palisades.

At last they came to Mixler Road and Broyles headed toward the sluice gate. At the turnoff leading up to the castle's parking lot, Thaddeus suddenly pulled over. He could proceed no further without being noticed by Broyles. But, parking at the crest of the final hill, he managed to walk south a hundred feet to where he could perfectly view the parking lot. He could just make out Broyles' motor scooter in the orange lights of the parking lot. The ride had been abandoned while Thaddeus walked from roadway to hilltop. He had lost sight of his quarry.

Thaddeus watched as a black limo arrived and a small man jumped out and jogged for the sluice gate. There he noticed a second man--Broyles?--who had been sitting in the grass. They exchanged a briefcase then returned to their vehicles. This time, Thaddeus hung back and fell in behind the black limousine. It wound around through the downtown of Washington with Thaddeus lagging far behind, when it suddenly sped up and headed for Virginia. They crossed the border and Thaddeus managed to follow the limo until it came to a long, curving driveway where it turned in and two men climbed out. Briefly, as the passenger paused under the porch light and sorted through his keychain, Thaddeus got a good look at Hoa's face. He committed it to memory. Now he had a face to connect to the caller who came on the line and said, "All the same."

Then he returned home.

He was congratulating himself as he opened a bottle of beer and slipped off his shoes in front of the TV. Bud was nowhere around. That was when it occurred to him: he should have snapped a picture of the exchange with a long-range lens. How excellent would that have been? He realized at that moment that he had started to think like a spy. Not only that, but he liked it.

He watched Wolf Blitzer on CNN talking about some election antics of one of the presidential candidates. As the TV rambled on and on, Thaddeus pulled his MacBook onto his lap and flipped it open. It made the WIFI connection and he waited for the browser to display his home page.

Then he clicked a link and logged into the office's network. The system would, of course, log his credentials and all details about this incursion, so he manipulated two text files to make it look as if he was logging-in on business. Then he brought up Broyles' calendar. He looked at that month's entries for the ninth day of June. Then the previous month's entries for the ninth day, going further and further back in time until the same entries on the ninth of those months were found no more.

All the same, each one said.

All the same.

~

JUST AFTER ELEVEN, his phone chimed. The name was blocked but he had a good idea who was calling.

"Thaddeus Murfee."

"Did you keep up with him?"

McGrant. He should have known she'd be all over him.

"I kept up."

"What did you see?"

"I didn't see much. He just went out to the reservoir."

"What did he do there?"

Thaddeus hesitated. She had told him to follow Broyles. But why wasn't the FBI there instead of him? That just didn't add up: he wasn't a trained agent; he had no idea how to spy on someone. He decided to wait before telling her. He needed more time, time to find someone he could confide in.

"He waited," Thaddeus said. "He waited around and then he left."

"Did you follow him after he left?"

"No."

"Why not?"

"You didn't tell me to. You told me to follow him out there."

"Jesus, Thaddeus."

"What?"

She exhaled a long, drawn-out sigh. He could imagine her face, the look she got when frustrated.

"That's it for now. We'll talk soon."

She hung up and left him smiling.

She would learn that he was no one's fool.

8

Bud Evans was a thick-legged soccer star from Odessa, Texas who roomed with Thaddeus and shared the same bathroom. Both men were in the small space Saturday night at six o'clock, making last-minute toilette refinements before going their separate ways on their separate dates.

Thaddeus' perplexed look caught Bud's attention.

"C'mon," said Bud, "you never look this extreme. Is it the girl you're meeting tonight or the new job? Give it up, Murf."

"Both," said Thaddeus as he held his round eyeglasses under warm water. "I've got to have dinner with my boss and try to charm the fam. That's all I can tell you; the rest of it is classified and if I breathe a word of it to you, I'll have to kill you."

"You and your scout troop," muttered Evans, pulling a wooden brush over the top of his head where the hair was long and then down the sides where the hair was clipped next to the scalp.

"Uh-huh," said Thaddeus. "I wish I could tell you. Well, this much I can tell, Buddy. My boss is probably going to be fired in the near future. I can't say why."

"Should you give a shit? I mean, he didn't even interview you, am I right?"

"That's right. I was hired through the Chief of Staff's office."

"So he's your boss in name only, correct?"

"I guess so. I mean I'm working in the office that has his name on it, though."

"You mean his name as the U.S. Attorney. I think it's more the generic U.S. Attorney's office than it is Broyles' office. His name's there only because the president appointed him."

"That's true. Okay, so let's say he gets shit-canned. That leaves me working for the administrative branch inside the office. But what's got me buffaloed," he said, turning to face his friend rather than his image in the mirror, "is that my boss is doing some shady stuff. There, I said it." Thaddeus looked nervously around. "I can't say what, so don't ask. But some very important people are keeping an eye on him. There, now I've said too much."

"No you haven't. We've been roomies for seven years now and I've never blabbed any of your bullshit to anyone else."

"Nor I yours. So we're even. Just make sure you keep your perfect record on this one. I'm going to jail if anyone finds out I even told you, Bud."

"Well, you didn't tell me. You intimated. Huge difference."

"God, law school fit you like a glove. Anyone who can split hairs that easily definitely belongs in the courtroom."

Evans faked a low bow. "Well, thank you, Thaddeus. Coming from the great hairsplitter himself, that pleases me to rank up there alongside you. So get down to it. What's he doing? Turning bad guys loose? Accepting bribes for not prosecuting? Letting bad guys out of prison? Come on, come on, come on, give it up."

Evans stopped and fixed his eyes on Thaddeus in the mirror.

"Last night, I saw my boss give a guy a briefcase," Thaddeus said.

Evans stopped brushing his hair. His hands fell to his sides. "What? That's it? A lawyer gave someone a briefcase? My God, how often does that happen?"

"All right, wiseass. It happened out at the reservoir, down by the sluice gate. In the dark."

Evans again stopped brushing. "Whoa! Selling secrets to the Russians? Is that where we are? But what secrets does a U.S. Attorney have? He's not in the secrets business. I think we're safe tonight," Evans laughed.

"Maybe turning over confidential documents about a prosecution?" guessed Thaddeus.

"Or maybe giving his CPA his canceled checks. Hell, I don't know. So what do you do about it?"

"I'm supposed to tell my handler."

"Who?"

"Melissa McGrant. She's who I'm actually reporting to."

"Hey, you know what?"

"What?"

"A sick thought just occurred to me. What if this bathroom is bugged? Or the living room? Or our phones? Shit, Murfee, get away from me, dog! You're radioactive!"

"Not gonna happen. I'm nothing to them," said Thaddeus. "I'm a nobody."

"Just the same, don't tell me anymore. I don't want to end up in front of some grand jury trying to explain what I was doing discussing your boss with you."

With that, Bud Evans left the bathroom.

Thaddeus came upright and began drying his eyeglasses.

"What the hell?" he said to his reflection. "What the hell?"

Two hours later, he was discussing attorney jobs with his boss's daughter, Nikki Broyles, over dessert at his boss's house.

"I never thought I'd be working as a prosecutor," he was telling Nikki, keeping his voice low enough that his boss--who was seated at the head of the table--wouldn't hear. After all, it wasn't entirely true that he was working as a prosecutor, but he hoped the charming Nikki didn't know. He hoped she imagined him as kind of a swashbuckling young lawyer going after the mafia or a sleeper cell. Answering her father's telephone would certainly spoil that image, but he wasn't about to tell her and was hopeful her father hadn't filled her in.

"I think it's pretty amazing," Nikki said. "If I go to law school, I'm looking for something in the government sector. Maybe

EPA. I like clean water, especially after what's been going on in Flint."

"Flint? Lots of elected officials to investigate out there. I'd convene a grand jury."

"Would you?" she smiled and pulled a strand of dark brown hair off her face and tucked it behind an ear. When she did, he noticed a large diamond ring on her left ring finger. His heart sank, as the view confirmed what he had thought earlier he had glimpsed there. *Damn,* he thought, *engaged? Why are the brainy ones already taken when I finally get to meet them? Not to mention gorgeous.*

"Would I investigate them? I'm sure someone already is. It's criminal and they should be punished."

She began, "My dad says--"

"Nikki!" her father interrupted. He was pointing a thick finger at her. "Can we leave Dad out of this?"

Thaddeus looked down at his plate, a disinterested someone who hadn't been listening. But he had, and her father knew it.

Nikki turned red and dropped her eyes to her plate. It was an uneasy moment.

"Hey," Thaddeus said, coming to her rescue, "how would you like to hit the zoo with me tomorrow? I've been looking for someone to take it in with me."

The National Zoo, he knew, charged no admission fee. It was free to one and all, and Thaddeus had used it before as a wooing location, given his financial state: always redlined on *dire*.

"I'd love to do that with you," she said. "Normally I study on Sundays but I can certainly afford a few hours off to see the pandas."

"You'll fall in love with the baby, Bei-Bei. Hey, you know they've got Panda-Cams where you can watch them live on your computer, right?"

She smiled brightly. "My, Murf, get out much?"

He had to laugh. "Can I tell you the truth?"

"Please do."

"The truth is, until I get paid on Friday I'm all but broke. A trip to a free zoo is the best I can offer anyone right now."

"You and me both. My dad gives me only so much money per semester and it has to last. I've already blown it on a new laptop and new stuff for my studio apartment. I'm just as broke as you, Murf."

"Well," he said slowly, "you could always sell that giant diamond on your hand."

She raised her hand to look at her diamond ring.

"That's all I have left of Charlie Macintyre. He was killed in Afghanistan. We were engaged."

"Jeez, I'm sorry," Thaddeus said. "I feel awful for saying that. Please forgive me."

"No, no, no, that's not necessary. I just haven't taken it off. I don't know if I ever will. We were very much in love. We were high school best friends and got engaged our sophomore year in college. Junior year he went to Afghanistan—Special Forces. I went to school. I never saw him again."

"Well, I feel like--I feel terrible and I'm sorry, so sorry."

"You couldn't have known, Murfee. It's all good."

She smiled and again brushed her longish hair from her face. It was an endearing struggle, keeping the strands of hair tucked behind the ears.

"So who are you supporting for president?" Thaddeus asked.

"Green Party. I'm Green Party, Greenpeace all the day. I'm also a card-carrying member of PETA."

"You want me to stop eating?" he asked, realizing that she hadn't eaten the baked chicken everyone else had enjoyed. It had been all salad and vegetables with her.

"No, I want everyone to stop eating chickens who've never seen the sun and never felt the earth beneath their feet. Caged-animals are tragic, Thaddeus. I hope you think so too."

"And I'm asking you to go to the zoo where every animal is caged."

"It's true. I don't believe in zoos. But I do want to see you again, let me be honest. What if we just went out for coffee, instead of the zoo?"

His face brightened. "That would be perfect. I can still afford an espresso."

"Done. Pick me up at six o'clock, please."

"It's a motor scooter. Bring a scarf."

"I'm not going to melt. Wind is fine."

"Done."

9

It was an older home, a Tudor on a quarter-acre two streets over from the Potomac. The young lawyer was impressed.

After dinner, Thaddeus was being taken on a tour of his boss's home by his boss's daughter, and now she had him outside, sitting beside her on a swing, talking. She went on and on about college and her dreams; he went on about law school and what it was like to finally graduate and at last cease from the endless briefing of cases that law school required. Fifteen minutes into their chat, her father appeared out of the dark and asked Thaddeus to walk with him.

"That's fine," said Nikki, "you've got fifteen minutes while I help mom in the kitchen. Thaddeus, keep your guard up with this guy."

Both men laughed; Thaddeus because he already had his guard up with Franklin J. Broyles.

They headed off on a sandy path that left the property and

skirted the next row of houses, winding up on the shoreline, where they began strolling silently through the dark at water's edge. At long last, Broyles cleared his throat and asked his question.

"Thaddeus, you took a call from one of our undercover agents. The one that said 'All the same.' Did anyone tell you we don't want those calls entered on our office diary?"

"No, sir. I thought everything went on the diary."

"Well, normally that would be true. But where there's no name and the message is 'all the same,' that's code for one of our most active undercover agents. He's wormed his way in with the Chinese and he's feeding us info."

"Are we prosecuting them?"

"Not them, per se, no. But they commit crimes in our jurisdiction on a regular basis. Cybercrimes, Thaddeus, and we're building a case against them. Several cases, in fact. One day--on orders from the President--we're going to issue indictments against them and expose the underbelly of Chinese cyber spying in our country. The District of Columbia is going to be the poster child for that campaign. Are you with me?"

"Yes, sir. All the way, sir. And by the way, cybercrime prosecution sounds exactly like what I want to get into. It's cutting-edge, it's important, and it's going to make or break our economy--our way of life--over the next ten years. I'd like to be there on the front lines, sir."

"Thaddeus, I'm glad you mentioned that. I've been thinking about you a lot lately, thinking about setting you up as an oversight leader. A liaison between me and the cybercrime staff. You would like that, wouldn't you?"

"I'd like it even more to be a prosecutor in that unit."

They paused and Broyles bent down and grabbed a few stones, which he began skipping across the evening water.

"That would certainly be on the horizon, too, Thaddeus. But here's what I really need you to help me with, right now."

"What's that?"

"My daughter. She seems to really like you."

"It's mutual. She's good people. I think we'll be good friends."

"And let's leave it at that, shall we? Friends? We don't ever want your official duties to bump up against my family, do we?"

"What do you mean, 'bump up against'?"

"Well, I wouldn't want anything at work to color how you might feel about Nikki."

"I don't know how that would ever happen."

Broyles turned to Thaddeus and nodded. "You know, I don't either. Let's forget what I just said. You two enjoy, get to know each other, and let an old man butt out. Nik's mother would kill me for even saying anything to you."

"It's all right, Mr. Broyles, I think I know what you were saying. I can't afford to allow feelings about you or your family to ever affect my work. That about it?"

"Bingo! Better than I could ever have said it."

"So I noticed," said Thaddeus with a laugh. "There won't be any problems, Mr. Broyles. I promise you."

Broyles moved a step closer.

"Truth-telling time?" said Broyles. "I think Nikki's lucky to meet you. You're top-flight, Thaddeus. I'm happy that she's getting to know you."

"Well, so far all we've done is enjoyed dinner together and reminisced about school, Mr. Broyles. It's not like we're picking out paint colors for our living room."

Broyles threw his head back and laughed heartily.

"Oh, that's good, Murf! That's rich!"

Thaddeus was feeling quite happy with the talk. He was finding his boss to be a charming, caring man. He was definitely having trouble reconciling what he saw at the sluice gate with the kind, informative man he was talking with right then. He became so at ease, in fact, that he weighed broaching the subject with Mr. Broyles. But, in the end, he decided it would be a damn stupid thing to do. In fact, though it was warm in the night air, he involuntarily shivered.

Damn stupid to bring it up, indeed.

10

Broyles knew from his days at the FBI that following a car at two o'clock in the morning without being discovered was difficult if not impossible. It was difficult because there was very little camouflage traffic around, at least on secondary roads. It wouldn't take the astute driver long to notice the tail, especially if the astute driver was meeting up with a Chinese spy ring, as Broyles was about to do. So the meet was set for early Sunday morning.

At two a.m. Sunday morning, Broyles drove his government Chrysler Sebring to an all-night Denny's Restaurant over from K Street. He did a cursory wait-and-see when he pulled in, leaving the motor running and moving slowly through the parking lot. When he was halfway confident he hadn't been followed, he parked and went inside and went straight through the building, through the kitchen, and out the back door, where he waited by a dumpster. Five minutes later, when no one had exited the back door after him, he retraced his steps, going back inside, where he grabbed a menu beside the cash register and scouted out a place to sit.

He found a deserted table at the far side of the counter, away from all windows, and slid his tray down the table to the chair beside the wall. It was as far away from the normal stream of commerce as he could get. Then he ordered and waited, thinking of what he was going to say to the man he was meeting. It had to be done in just the right way.

His food came. Ever so slowly, he dined. When he was finished, he waited. And waited. No waitress. He went up to the counter, refilled his cup, and returned to his table to wait again. At long last, he peeled off a twenty and laid it on the table. Then he went back through the kitchen and passed by the dumpsters until he came to a high hedge bordering the rear property line and he sat down on the curb there.

At four a.m., headlights swung around to the back of the restaurant, yellow shafts of light passed across the waiting Broyles and then beamed at the far side of the lot as the vehicle straightened out before stopping. A lone figure got out on the passenger side and approached. He sat down beside Broyles and stared straight ahead.

"You were followed Friday night," said the second man. A match flared and his features were briefly illuminated. The face of Sing Di Hoa turned to the side and waited.

Broyles didn't look over. "Followed? You're sure of this?"

"Definite."

"Who?"

"Your new man. Thaddeus Murfee."

"What did he see?"

"We think he saw everything. He stopped and parked his

motor scooter one hundred meters from our exchange. It isn't good. Who is he working for?"

Broyles felt as if he had been kicked in the gut. It hadn't occurred to him that Thaddeus Murfee was working for anyone except him. But that wasn't entirely true. Frank, the custodian at the office, had also mentioned that he came upon Murfee inside Broyles' office, doing who knows what. Frank had also presented him with a tiny listening device, a bug. All government offices were bugged and the appearance of another of the devices was not a big event; rather, it was even commonplace. Still, Broyles should have paid more attention to the fact the kid was new and he didn't know him all that well instead of thinking the intrusion innocent. Innocent, hell; now it was looking like Murfee was all over him.

"Who's he working for? That would be hard to say. Maybe FBI."

"So we get rid of him, plain and simple."

"If I'm being watched, getting rid of him doesn't solve our problem. He's reported what he saw."

"There is that," said the Chinese man.

"So what do we do?"

"I am to tell you that your usefulness has come to an end, Mr. Broyles. We won't be trading with you again."

"Now hold on!" Broyles hissed in the darkness. "That isn't right and you people goddamn well know it isn't right. I've never been anything but true blue to you. I've come too far to quit now. If I quit now they might just blow it up and come after me with everything they've got. We've got to make it look like we're still doing business until I can set myself free."

"How would you do that?"

"Disappear. Europe, probably. South America, maybe. But I need time to set it up."

"We understand that. We're prepared to continue meeting. But we won't be paying you anymore and we won't be expecting anything from you. Is this understood?"

"Then I need a cash-out package. I need a cash-out package or I blow it up myself. Turn government rat and come clean on it all. I could do Witness Protection. Or, I need ten million from you and safe passage to the country of my choosing plus new ID."

The cigarette flared as Hoa inhaled. He took another drag and then stubbed it out. He nodded, finally.

"My people will agree to that. It's not new."

"Then we'll have a clean break. Which is all I want. Now what about this Murfee?"

"We're prepared to deal with him."

"In what way?"

Hoa smiled. He reached around and clasped Broyles on the shoulder.

"That is definitely none of your concern. Within the week, Mr. Murfee will no longer be working for you. He won't be working anywhere."

Broyles went silent. He sat, looking ahead. Nikki was on his mind. She liked the guy.

"Let's wait on that," said Broyles as thoughtfully as he knew how. "Let me size this up before you simply take him out. I know the FBI and if Thaddeus Murfee is killed they will be all over it. You would be stirring up a hornet's nest, Hoa. Can you get your people to give me some time with it?"

Hoa looked ahead. Then he nodded. "We'll wait. But not for long." The smaller man stood and shook out the kinks. "We'll meet again next month."

Hoa walked back to his waiting car. When he was gone, Broyles sat alone in the dark for a good ten minutes, thinking. He had much to do. Preparations had to be made. He would be giving up everything he loved--Jeannette, Nikki, the boys--but he had always known it could come to that, one way or the other. He had hoped for a clean death and a Swiss account for Jeannette. But who could tell, maybe he had outlived his usefulness to the Chinese and they would take *him* out. Or maybe his own government would do him in now that his usefulness was coming to an end. They could murder him, or they could claim he was a spy and maybe prosecute him for treason—the permutations were almost endless. It took everything he had to fight back the regret that said suicide was his only way out.

He then stood and rubbed a backhand across his eyes. Thinking of Jeannette had filled them with tears. Thinking of leaving her--and the kids—he shivered hard and fought to pull himself together. He pulled out a handkerchief and mopped his cheeks. Then he walked around to his car, got in, and drove home.

This time he paid no attention to tails. His life was about to change forever in ways over which he had no control and being found out was honestly the least of his worries. Was he ready for the coming change—that was the only worry that mattered.

His brain said he was. But his gut said otherwise. And with a sob he went inside his house, climbed upstairs, and stole into bed, where he drew Jeannette close to him and rested his head against her shoulder.

He held her and wept until dawn.

She never knew a thing.

11

Whether Thaddeus would tell McGrant about Broyles' reservoir meeting--or not--was decided early Monday morning when her car pulled in front of Thaddeus on M Street. Her front tires forced his scooter to the curb. Now her driver had him hemmed in, unable to move, so he jumped off the scooter and walked around to the driver's side of the offending car. It was a black Lincoln Town Car, one up front, one in back. Then he saw: McGrant. He was immediately angry at her for the dangerous maneuver. He decided to say nothing about the meeting Friday night at the reservoir. First he needed to figure out where he stood in all this. He rapped his knuckles hard on her window. It came down.

"What the hell, Ms. McGrant?" he said. "That was really bad."

"We need to speak. Get in."

"No way. I'm parked in a red zone. My scooter will get taken away."

"Get in."

"Look, I don't mind going with you, but I'm not leaving my scooter. Follow me back to my apartment and we'll go from there."

Without another word, he climbed on his scooter, waited for her car to give him room, and began the ten minute ride home. Her vehicle followed and then pulled alongside him in his designated parking slot at the apartment building.

"Get in," she said again.

This time he obliged her, climbing in on the driver's side, backseat. The car began backing out, raced through the parking lot, and swept away into morning traffic.

"What the hell?" Thaddeus said, still angry at her.

"Get over it. I need you to come with me."

"I can't. I'm due at work in twenty minutes."

"It can wait. Take out your cell phone and call your office. Tell them you're running late because you have to stop by your doctor's office. Or not. Tell them whatever you want. But make it sound legitimate."

He did as she said, making up a song and dance about a broken tooth and a trip to a dentist.

They wound through rush hour traffic, making their way downtown where they pulled inside a nondescript industrial building. The gate closed behind them as Thaddeus looked back over his shoulder. Conversation between the two had been non-existent as they rode along in silence.

"Where are we?" Thaddeus asked.

"This is an FBI station. You'll see."

"FBI? In this falling-down building?"

"Hang loose, Mr. Murfee."

The car lurched ahead and began following a typical parking-garage tunnel that wound its way down and down. Thaddeus guessed they were maybe three floors below street level when they abruptly came to a stop. McGrant opened her door and looked over at him. "We get off here."

He followed her to a bank of elevators, where she inserted a keycard and punched a button. He felt his stomach rise as they rode even deeper into the bowels of the building.

They came to a stop at what must have been five floors below their parking level. The doors slid open and Thaddeus found himself in an enormous room much larger than the ground-level footprint of the building upstairs.

"Someone's been busy," he opined.

"FBI devices are created, built, and tested here. That's why we've come. You are going to learn how to hide a camera."

Thaddeus groaned. A camera?

She led him to a partitioned area open on the entrance side. They were met by a man with white hair who was wearing blue coveralls that said *FBI* above the breast pocket. An ID card dangled from a cord around his neck. No introductions were made.

"Mr. Murfee," said the man, "step over here and have a seat at my work table."

Thaddeus did as instructed. McGrant took the chair next to his.

"This," said the man, holding up an object the size of a pencil eraser, "is a very powerful wide-angle camera. It is built to be inserted into pictures of the president."

"Come again?" said Thaddeus. "Why would you have a camera designed for the president's picture?"

The man smiled. "Because all government offices are required by law to have pictures of the sitting president in all key public areas. Your handler, Ms. McGrant, has selected an office where you will install this same model."

Thaddeus looked at McGrant. She smiled. He shook his head.

"Sorry, but I'm not installing a camera in Mr. Broyles' office, if that's where we're going with this."

"You're refusing an order from your supervisor?" asked McGrant in a cold, no-nonsense voice. "Think how that would look on your résumé."

She was right. Keeping something like that off his work history was very motivating.

"All right," he said with a sigh. "Show me what to do."

An hour later, he had it down. And he had the micro-camera and a small coring blade and a tube of cement as well.

"Any questions?"

"Pretty straightforward," Thaddeus replied.

McGrant allowed a slight smile. "See? You'll make a fine spy yet."

They rode the elevator back up to the parking level, where they climbed back into her car. They surfaced and exited the building.

"All right," Thaddeus said as they swung back into traffic, "this all seems very random. Am I allowed to know what we're doing here?"

"You weren't listening for the past hour? You're planting a camera."

"Yeah, but why?"

She touched the side of her head. "Need to know, Mr. Murfee. Need to know."

"You're going to have to do better than that. What do you expect to find out with this camera?"

"We need to attach faces to voices. The bugs inside his office only give us voice. We need video as well. We're going to bust his ass and we need video for the jury. Does that do it for you?"

He turned toward his window. A minute later, he turned back.

"Why aren't you using FBI agents to plant the camera? Why use me?"

"FBI agents have a security protocol to follow just like everyone else when coming and going from governmental buildings. Their access and egress is logged. We can't risk that, not where the agents didn't actually have a purpose for coming into his offices. He could track them down."

"So it's my problem."

"Who else would you suggest we use, Mr. Murfee? You're right outside his door."

"Speaking of, there's a maintenance man, name of Frank, who's warned me about going into Broyles' office when Broyles isn't there."

"Frank? We'll move him out. Not to worry."

Thaddeus stared ahead. "Good enough."

They rode in silence for another three miles. At last she spoke.

"Tomorrow's payday. Where's all the money going to go?"

"Rent. A decent meal out. I've got a friend to take to dinner."

"Would that be Nikki?"

"You know about Nikki? Are you people watching every step I take?"

"Yes we are. Don't get too close to her. It's only going to come out bad."

"Why? She's not involved in any of this."

"No, but you are. And when she finds out your role in her father's imprisonment she's going to hate you with every cell in her body. We know her and we know how she'll respond."

"That isn't right. You never said anything about interfering in my personal life."

"Mr. Murfee, when you agreed to spy, you didn't agree to just a part of your life being involved. You agreed to a job that might not be to your liking all the time. No job ever is. I'm just asking you to put the brakes on where Broyles' daughter is concerned."

The young lawyer had no response. This was all new. A real unexpected twist was that he wasn't sure anymore where he stood legally. Was what he was doing even legal? Spying on a U.S. Attorney? He'd started having serious doubts since the sluice gate. Maybe it was time to hire a lawyer of his own. He would have the money to do that tomorrow. He would make some calls today. It was time to stand up for himself. He had to admit he was very young and inexperienced. But he wasn't stupid.

No one had ever said that about him.

12

Friday rolled around--payday at long last. So Thaddeus visited a lawyer.

John Henry Fitzhugh was a garrulous, fifty-something lawyer who kept offices in the Watergate Office Building on the ground floor--the most expensive real estate in all of Washington. Fitzhugh was lean and lanky, a varsity volleyball player at Cornell, and a member of the Order of the Coif, which was an honorary fraternity at NYU law. His face was finely chiseled with a long, hawkish nose, and a mouth that was always moving, always speaking. Thaddeus liked him immediately upon entering into his office, shaking the man's hand, and taking a seat as instructed.

"Call me Fitz," he told Thaddeus. "Want a beer? Coffee?"

"I'm good, thanks."

Fitzhugh ran a hand back over his close-cropped graying hair. He pushed the steel rim glasses up on his nose and folded his hands on his desk.

"All right, then. Tell me what brings you here, Mr. Murfee."

"Thaddeus."

"All right, Thaddeus. What troubles are you bringing to me?"

"I'm being used."

"Aren't we all?" said Fitzhugh with a laugh that burst out like pigeons scattering. "Hell, everyone's using all of us. Why is your case different?"

"The government gave me a job and didn't tell me up front that I was going to spy for them."

"Oh, slow down! The U.S. Government got you involved in spying?"

"That's what I'm saying."

"Where do you work?"

"U.S. Attorney's office."

"Broyles? You work for Frank Broyles and he got you into spying?"

"I work for him but I was hired by a woman named Melissa McGrant."

"Go ahead and tell me all of it."

Thaddeus went into every detail, start to finish, from the initial job interview to yesterday, when he had been taken to the FBI devices lab and taught how to install a video camera. While he went on and on, his new attorney listened attentively, lips pursed, taking it in. By the time he was finished, Fitzhugh had interrupted with questions a half-dozen times and Thaddeus had wound up telling him everything he could think of.

"Let me see if I understand, Thaddeus. The government evidently believes that Frank Broyles is selling state secrets. Or at least some kind of secrets. Do you know why they believe this? Has anyone ever told you?"

Thaddeus' expression changed. Searching back over his meetings with McGrant, he honestly couldn't think of any instance where she had told him why his government thought Frank Broyles was a traitor. It just hadn't come up in that context. And he hadn't told her about the Broyles reservoir meeting and didn't plan to. At least not yet. But he did tell Mr. Fitzhugh, who looked troubled.

"That was a huge risk you took in going to the reservoir. You're not trained for anything like that."

"I know. I had no business doing that."

"They're just using you, Thaddeus. In the worst possible way, without a thought for your own safety."

“I'm their dupe.”

Fitzhugh ignored that. “So here's the first thing I want you to do. I want you to confront Ms. McGrant. Find out from her exactly what they have on Broyles. It seems to me you're entitled to know that."

"She'll say I'm not. She keeps reminding me I'm 'need to know'.”

"Then threaten to go to the papers. Threaten to turn them all over if they don't let you in on what's going on. As your lawyer, I don't want you participating in something like this, one. But two, if you have been tricked into it, I want to know why they're doing it at all. Just saying he's up to no good isn't enough. We need facts to support your actions. Real facts, not just some 'need to know' kind of bullshit. Okay?"

"Okay."

"The third thing is, if this stuff is on the up-and-up, you could be at risk. At serious risk of who knows what? Spies have been known to get whacked. I'm not saying that's what you're up against here, but it has been known to happen. So I'm going to suggest you demand FBI protection while you're working for her. There's no reason you shouldn't have it."

"I don't like the idea of being followed by the FBI but I like even less the idea that I'm going to be followed by the Chinese or whoever. That scares the hell out of me."

"As it should."

"What else?"

"Hazardous duty pay. They're not paying you enough. I want you to demand a raise. What they're paying, for someone doing what you're doing, is about half of what you should be getting. Let's have you demand three-hundred and see what happens. Fair enough?"

"I'll do it. So let me see if I have this straight. First thing, find out what they know about Broyles. Second thing, FBI protection. Third thing, more money. Speaking of which, how much will I be paying you?"

Fitzhugh sat back in his chair and leveled his gaze at Thaddeus. "Fact is, Thaddeus," he began slowly, "you can't afford to pay me anything. At least not yet. I'll keep my hours and we can settle up when you're earning what you should be earning. Until then, let's not worry about it. I'll invoice you every month so you know where we are, but I won't expect payment until we both agree it's time. Does this work for you?"

Waves of relief washed over him. He knew coming in that he couldn't afford a lawyer who had an office on the ground floor of the Watergate. He knew he needed this, an older man to bounce ideas off. He'd never had it before and he felt good about John Henry Fitzhugh. Of course, the price would be sky high, but his advisor at Georgetown Law had told him to see Fitzhugh. He had steered Thaddeus the right way, evidently, because the man was tough and he was willing to work with him on fees. Thaddeus' spirit lifted. For the first time in weeks he felt a little hope.

"One last thing," Thaddeus said. "What do I do about the camera? McGrant expects me to install it on Broyles' picture of the president. It's hanging right inside his office, right beside his desk. I've already scoped it out and I know I could do it. I'd probably be in and out in less than five minutes. Do I go ahead with it?"

Fitzhugh frowned. "Why did they say they needed a camera on him?"

Thaddeus spread his hands. "They want to catch him committing a crime. Selling secrets or something. They need faces, not just voices, because they're going to take it to a jury."

"Take it to a jury? Sounds like they're getting ready to indict him. Take it in front of the grand jury. I can't be certain from what you're saying. This is a tough one, Thaddeus, and I'm not positive I know the answer. I mean, if you get caught at it, and if the FBI and McGrant should disavow knowledge of what you were up to, you would be in very serious trouble. You could be facing federal charges that would wind you up in prison for twenty years."

"I won't do it, then."

"Hold on. Hold on. Let's think it through. First, you have McGrant who told you this was all approved. The DOJ is implicated, too. What I'm going to suggest is that we get McGrant on record. Maybe a video cam or at least audio of her telling you to do this thing. You need to have that in your pocket in case this all blows up. Knowing these folks like I do, and knowing how political it all is, you would be the first casualty if they got a tit in a wringer. They'd hang you out to dry in a second. So let's get her recorded."

"How do I do that?"

"Let's talk about it."

Twenty minutes later, they had their plan of protection. Thaddeus wasn't sure it would work, and he wasn't sure it was enough, but he was beginning to trust John Henry Fitzhugh literally with his life. He had to: he didn't have anywhere else to turn.

When he left, he knew what he needed.

He rode his scooter to a nearby sandwich shop and went inside. He ordered a turkey on rye, sea salt chips and a diet Coke. Food in hand, he grabbed a small table off by himself. Then he took out his phone and began browsing online. Within minutes he found the ad he had known would be out there:

> *PROFESSIONAL STEALTH HIDDEN CAMERA EXECUTIVE PEN - PLUG & PLAY into any PC/Mac. Simply record your footage, plug the spy pen into your computer with the included USB cable, and review your footage. That's all it takes! User friendly and a complete no-brainer to use. Spy This, 9-9 today. Metro D.C.*

That's me, he thought. *A complete no-brainer for ever getting myself into this.*

He fired up his Vespa and rode across town to the store named Spy This. He plunked down $59.95 plus tax and left with a camera pen capable of recording ninety minutes of video with audio. Which was all good. But there it stopped. It stopped because that left him with five dollars and change. Every last cent he had in the world.

But on the bright side, it was Friday. He would be paid that afternoon and he was so ready.

So ready.

13

$3 *209.22* the paycheck said. And it was drawn on the U.S. Treasury, so he knew it was good.

After work, Thaddeus climbed on his scooter and visited the Bank of America on Pennsylvania Avenue. The inside of a bank had never looked so good to him before. Thaddeus queued up and ten minutes later was standing at the teller window. A deposit slip was ready. He received $500 cash back. That was meant to last him two weeks for personal use, according to his new budget. He carefully folded the five bills and put them inside his left front trouser pocket. He patted the pocket, felt the outline of the bills, and folded his receipt and put that inside his shirt pocket. *All is well with Thaddeus Murfee's financial picture*, he thought as he walked outside to his Vespa. Now to go meet McGrant after hours.

The Petri Dish bar and grill was located just two blocks north of where Thaddeus parked his scooter every day, so he used the employees' parking lot at the U.S. Attorney's building and walked on up. In his breast pocket was the brand new spy pen, switched on, its blue light glowing on the user's side. The light wouldn't be seen from the subject's side. McGrant had agreed to meet him at six sharp.

He arrived at the bar and grill, went inside and found a booth, and filled a basket with peanuts. Munching happily, he rehearsed how he would try to get an admission out of McGrant that she had hired him to spy.

At 6:10 she still hadn't arrived and Thaddeus was just a little concerned. She wanted the FBI camera hidden in Broyles' office by Monday closing, so he was left with little time to get her on video before he went along with her plan. For his part, Thaddeus still wasn't entirely sure why the FBI couldn't hide its own damn camera, but apparently that was not open to discussion. The job was his and she meant for him to do it without further delay.

At 6:15 she came straggling in lugging a stuffed briefcase, wind-blow hair across her face in wisps, and blowing a stream of air out of her mouth to move the hair away from her eyes. She spied Thaddeus' raised hand and promptly came over to the booth he had commandeered.

"Thaddeus," she said, and held out her hand.

They shook hands. The place was rocking out its newly installed sound system and the music was deafening. He knew they would have to shout but was concerned it would all be lost on his spy pen. The instructions, however, said the digital works of the pen included a background noise filter so he was hopeful it was industrial strength enough to record her.

The cocktail waitress took their orders. Both were sticking with non-alcoholic, her with Perrier and him with Diet

Coke. Never one to beat around the bush, McGrant opened first.

"So, Thaddeus, why is it that you just had to see me today?" She folded her hands on the table and sat motionless, fully at ease, waiting.

"We got paid today."

"I'll bet that's a relief."

"It is--was. But it also raised a bit of an alarm for me."

"Which is?"

"I need a raise. I need more take-home pay if I'm ever going to whittle down my student loans."

"How much are they after you for?"

"Two-fifty and change."

"Two hundred and fifty thousand dollars in law school loans? Holy shit!"

"Not all is law school. About fifty is undergrad."

"So how much are your payments going to be now that you've graduated?"

"About four grand a month," he lied. It was all prepared, what he was telling her. He had pushed the numbers around on his calculator and come up with a pretty decent tale of woe.

"Four grand? And how much do you take home?"

"About thirty-two-hundred every other Friday. Which means one full check plus part of the second will be going to pay student loans. I can't live on what's left."

"You can, Thaddeus, you just don't want to." She abruptly raised a hand when he started to object. "Let me finish, please. I was going to say I don't blame you. You're working way too many hours for what you're actually going to be seeing as disposable income. I get it."

"I'm glad you do. I was hoping to stay on with the U.S. Attorney but I was beginning to worry I might have to resign and go with a firm that pays more."

"Third in your class, that shouldn't be that hard to do. But let's do this. Let me tentatively say we'll bump you up to two hundred a year. I know I can get that done; it's in our budget. Does that work?"

Thaddeus stole a look down at the blue light on the back of the spy pen. He prayed it was getting all this.

"That works. That's very generous and will make all the difference in how I can afford to live. This city is so damn expensive I didn't know what else to do but come to you. I can't even get an apartment from what I have left even an hour out of town. So it's huge. Besides, I'll bet you can't hire many spies for what you're paying me. Am I right?"

Just then the drink order arrived. Thaddeus laid a hundred-dollar bill on the table.

"Right back with change," said the young cocktail waitress.

McGrant seemed not to have heard his question, so he plunged ahead.

"I was saying, I'll bet it's hard to get someone to spy--"

"I heard that, Thaddeus. Heard that. I don't know what you

want me to say. What's done is done. Let's change the subject."

Damn, he thought. *She must be onto me.* They lapsed into small talk, then, going over the presidential race that was dragging into its second year and making the entire country crazy with the campaign commercials and the vile things the candidates were claiming about each other. Yes, they were tired of that. Everyone was. Then Thaddeus tried again.

"Incidentally, I scoped out Broyles' office where you want me to hide the camera. I think I can do it in five minutes or less."

"Five minutes? Great! I'm sure you're pleased with yourself."

"You are still wanting me to go ahead with it, aren't you?"

"Thaddeus, are you recording me?"

"Not at all! I just want to make sure I know what I'm doing!"

"Good. Let's change the subject, shall we? In fact, we've got your take-home pay dilemma resolved so I think I'll just be on my way."

She stood to leave.

"Thanks for the drink. We'll do it again sometime, Thaddeus."

"You're welcome. Thanks for coming, Ms. McGrant."

"So long."

He sat there for ten long minutes, just staring. She had sniffed him out. She had uncovered his plot and blown him away.

Then he thought of Nikki. It would be good to hang with someone his own age, someone who was on his team--as far as he knew. So he called her up.

"Hey," she said. "What's up, Thaddeus?"

"I'm down here at *The Petri Dish* thinking about you. Wanta drop by and knock back a few with me?"

"Sure. I'm finishing up a psych paper. Can you give me forty-five minutes?"

"I'll be waiting. So long, lady."

"Keep the lights on."

~

SHE ARRIVED at half past eight. By that time, Thaddeus had downed two draft beers and shot two rounds of pool. Plus, he had bought a round of drinks for the players at his pool table. He was happy and charming by the time Nikki walked up and tapped him on the shoulder.

"Let's sit down," she yelled above the sound system. "We need to talk."

"I'm down with that," he said. "And I just saw a table open up. Hurry!"

A two-chair table with wire legs and a round green top had been vacated. Nikki turned and made her way to it just as two young professionals in suits and ties reached it too.

"After you, Miss," said the friendly, youthful black man. He held out a hand, indicating Nikki should sit down. Thaddeus swooped in right behind her and the two young men laughed and went off looking for another perch in the bar.

"Well," she said, and gave the waitress her order.

"I'm good," Thaddeus said. "My limit is three beers in three hours or I fall off my motor scooter."

"Are you looking for a car now that you're making the big bucks?"

He shrugged. "I honestly don't know. Truth is, I don't really feel like getting all caught up with car payments right now. That seems a little risky."

She smiled and wrinkled up her nose. "Don't be silly! Third in your class? Everyone wants to hire you, Thad. You're fresh meat."

"I am? I'm already feeling like an old worn-out shoe."

"Is my dad that hard on you, really?"

He looked away from her. "It's not just that. Just a lot of stuff going on. Forgive me, Nik, I'm not really supposed to be talking about it."

"Well, let's change the subject, shall we? Let's talk about constitutional law."

"Let's not and say we did. How about we talk about getting away together Saturday night. Holing up in some grand hotel and watching videos all night."

She surveyed him with her head tilted back.

"That's it? Videos is the best you can do?"

"Well," he said. "If anything else develops, so be it."

"I'm not that kind of girl, Thaddeus Murfee," she said coyly.

"Really? What kind are you?"

"I'm the kind who thought you'd never ask! I'd love to spend Saturday night with you at some swank hotel. Or in the park. Or at the zoo. Or in that little apartment you told me about, the one where the roommates' beds bang against the walls all night. Now *that's* romantic."

He laughed and couldn't stop. Then, "I like a girl who knows what she wants."

She smiled sheepishly. "Well, Mr. Murfee, I happen to like a guy who has what I want."

"What might that be?"

"Style and grace. You're a good guy, Murf. My dad is lucky to have you taking care of him."

Thaddeus was unable to respond. *If she only knew,* he was thinking. *I'm about to take her dad down, help put him in prison, and she's grateful he has me. OMG!*

There was a lull. Then she spoke up. "Did I say something wrong about my dad? He is lucky to have you, isn't he?"

"Absolutely," Thaddeus lied, and hated himself for lying. What the hell was he even thinking, preparing to spend the night with the daughter of the man he was going to help put in prison. It wasn't right and she would hate him for it if it happened. Plus he would feel like he had used her. Used her to satisfy himself--he hadn't been with a girl in six months. Not having any money had turned him into a stay-at-home curmudgeon, as he saw it. And now his chance to have fun and frolic in the hay had come around and he was on a self-inflicted guilt trip.

"So let's do this," he continued. "How about I check a few things at the office in the morning and then I call to confirm tomorrow night?"

Her face fell. "What, we can't confirm now?"

"Oh, you know how it is. I'm just always nervous something's going to come in at the last minute and wreck my plans. I'm really on-call twenty-four/seven."

"You are? My dad didn't say anything about that."

"Well, there're probably a few things like that which are on the down-low. Hours and times and salaries--it's all pretty hush-hush with the feds."

She leaned back and brushed a length of hair back from her face.

"That's for sure. My dad complains about DOJ oversight constantly. People think U.S. Attorneys have total autonomy, but they really don't. There's always someone to answer to."

"I guess law is always like that. If it's not the government, it's the bar association. Those people are always breathing down your neck."

"That doesn't sound like great fun," she said.

Nikki's drink order arrived--finally--and Thaddeus threw a ten-dollar bill on the table.

"Flush are we?" she chided him.

He blushed. "We are. Finally."

"So what to buy first?"

"First? Tomorrow afternoon I'm going shopping for sheets for my bed. I haven't had any sheets since I started law school."

"You must be joking!"

"Luxurious sheets. What color do you like?"

"Black."

"Black sheets it is. Hopefully we'll get to break them in."

She leaned in and smiled. "Why wouldn't we?"

He shrugged. "We will. If my luck holds."

"You don't need luck, Thaddeus. You've got me."

14

Later Friday night, Sing Di Hoa met Broyles in the same restaurant parking lot as before.

"You needed to hear this without delay," said the smaller man. Broyles would describe the man's eyes as fiery, later that night when he recalled their meeting. Hoa was definitely onto something.

"My daughter met Mr. Murfee tonight. Is that what this is about?"

"We eavesdropped on their conversation. But even before he met your daughter, he met with Melissa McGrant."

"Melissa McGrant?"

"Yes. He said she was trying to get him to plant a video camera in your office."

Broyles was startled but not surprised. First the young lawyer had followed them, and now a video camera.

"I say we do nothing," said Broyles. "If we react or if we

remove the camera then we've put them on notice that we're onto them. Not good, Mr. Hoa."

"Exactly," said Hoa. "We want you to continue as usual in your office. But we also need to make sure there are no inadvertent statements by you that could come back to haunt. Or, worse, blow our cover, as you Americans say. We don't want our cover blown."

"Of course not. And it won't be. I can promise you that."

Hoa frowned. "There's something else, too. Some of my superiors want you gone."

Broyles' heart leapt in his chest. *Want you gone?* He thought. *What the hell did that mean?*

"Want me gone? You're wanting me to vanish already?"

"Let me be perfectly open with you, Mr. Broyles. Yes, some want you to vanish. And there are some who wish you dead. Only then will they be comfortable that you won't blow it up between us. You've threatened to do that, you know."

"But that was just commentary!" Broyles protested. "I wouldn't ever actually do that."

"Still, I had to report what you said. My best advice to you? Pack your toothbrush and vanish."

"What about the money I need? What about the ten million you promised?"

"It will be there. Your account in the Cayman Islands will receive a deposit by Monday afternoon. After that, we all want you gone."

"So be it, then," Broyles said. He had to agree. The alternative course of action if he failed to agree was unacceptable. Just for a moment he felt a flutter of hope: might Jeannette come with him? Then he remembered Jeannette. Poor, plodding Jeannette. She'd never had a love of adventure. She'd never go along with leaving her life behind. But so what? There were other women in the world. More desirable ones, as well. But that left Nikki and her brothers. It would be all but impossible to leave them behind. Whatever; he would cross that bridge later on. There would be some way to contact the kids once he got settled into his new life. He saw no reason why they couldn't work something out.

"So you'll leave?"

Broyles leaned forward on the curb and shielded his eyes from a passing car.

"As you say, I'll vanish. Be gone by Tuesday night."

"Excellent. Then I'll report that back. Our friends will be happy to hear."

Broyles suddenly shivered. "Just keep them away from me, Hoa. Can you promise me that?"

"Consider it done. You cooperate and there won't be a problem. I promise you that."

"Yes." Broyles knew in the world of espionage there were no promises. Words meant nothing. Only consequences counted. Actions and reactions--that was how you knew your enemy's mind.

Enemy. Indeed, it had come around to that. The Chinese were no longer his partners. They were now his number one enemy. He would act accordingly.

When they were done, Broyles climbed onto his Piaggio and threaded through stop-and-go traffic. Then he maneuvered across town to a seedy little apartment complex across from an industrial park. He went around back and parked in the alley. He crept up to the unit on the corner and let himself inside.

Home. Really? It had actually come down to just him and an apartment one step above a flophouse?

But it was furnished. Furnished and rented to Jackson L. Streeter.

Previously known as Franklin J. Broyles.

15

F Street is all that separates the U.S. Attorney's office from the FBI headquarters in Washington. It is a somewhat busy street, one that is carefully surveilled from strategic locations in the area for vehicles that might try to detonate a bomb on either side.

It was Monday morning and McGrant was setting up her day. She watched as FBI agent Naomi Ranski crossed F Street on her way over.

So far, it hasn't happened and we have been lucky, thought Melissa McGrant, staring out her third floor window. Her thoughts focused on the specter of China and Russia and North Korea and Iran. The time had arrived; McGrant saw it every day: cyberattacks, cybercrime, intrusions and data theft. Plus, out and out terror. Thousands of agents knew it was only a matter of time before federal buildings in the nation's capital would be incinerated by the next generation of explosive devices. They were coming. She turned away from her office window feeling overwhelmed. But she had an idea, a tiny chink in China's armor. It wasn't much, but it was a place to start. With the FBI's lead, of course.

McGrant's job was to protect American citizens. In doing so she was a true warrior through and through. Would she hesitate to spy on any government official if she believed they were out to do harm to the country? Not one second would she hesitate. In fact, this morning she was preparing to prove that, as she considered with the FBI what to do about Franklin J. Broyles and his Chinese comrades now that they had been photographed exchanging a briefcase. It was the smoking gun they had needed. Beyond that, what came after Broyles was locked up? She had her ideas about that. Hopefully, Ranski would agree.

What Broyles had been up to--what secrets had been passed off--was known. The DOJ and FBI had their methods. There had been the handoff at the reservoir sluice gate. And there had been two more meetings between the players since that night, both in the backlot of a local restaurant. The two additional meetings had not included exchanges of any kind, so the FBI was speculating that those two meetings were planning sessions. Broyles wasn't talking to anyone about any of it so McGrant and Ranski were out of that loop. But something was about to break and the FBI meant to be out ahead of it.

McGrant's receptionist gave a half-smile and nod as Ranski passed by. Ranski entered McGrant's inner office without bothering to knock. They went way back and long ago had established how they worked together. Knocking was no longer required.

Ranski tossed a manila envelope onto McGrant's desk. McGrant looked up in question.

"Surveillance," said Ranski. "Hoa and Broyles. Taken from across the street and from the rooftop."

"Where?"

"Denny's Restaurant."

"Anyone make your people?"

Ranski looked at her old confidante with a half-sneer. "You kidding?"

"All right, then. Let's see what we have."

McGrant slid the dozen photographs out of the envelope.

"Arriving, leaving. What the hell is Broyles riding?"

"Three-wheeled scooter. That's how he's losing our people in traffic, filtering up to stop lights between lanes of stand-still traffic."

"So?"

"So we've got a helicopter. He never looks up."

"I'm guessing his engine drowns it out."

"No one ever said he was into the world of spy craft. Most of the time he doesn't even bother looking behind himself. It's easy-peasy for our guys."

"What else?"

Ranski opened a second folder. "These are shots of the meeting at the reservoir. Broyles handing off his briefcase to Hoa."

"Was Thaddeus Murfee able to follow him?"

"He did. He observed all this from a distance."

"The little bastard never told me about seeing it. He's holding out on me."

"So he can't be trusted."

"Yes and no. He was able to follow Broyles and that's saying something since your guys have lost him more than once. But you're right, I don't like that he hasn't confided in me. But you know what? I think that's more a matter of convincing him we're the good guys. Frank Broyles has probably got him half-convinced that he's the good guy. So let's think in terms of making him certain who the players are and who the white hats are."

"It's worth a try," said Ranski. "But I don't like him not telling you. I call bullshit on that."

McGrant shook her head. "Noted. Now, what else do we have here?" She was referring to the Broyles-Hoa photos.

"That's it. Photos of all meetings. It's time to take him down."

McGrant looked up from the photos. She said, "We've got them meeting twice since the reservoir. I get that. And here's the proof, the photos. I get that, too. And we've got the reservoir shots. So what do you want me to do, indict him?"

"That's exactly what I want you to do."

"Game over if we do that. We don't get to know what they're up to if we ice Broyles."

"It's time. We've gotten all we're going to get from their little tête-à-têtes. It's time to close the noose."

"You're sure this is what you want, Agent Ranski?"

"When can you get it done?"

"By Tuesday afternoon."

"We'll be waiting for the paperwork. U.S. Marshals will pick him up. No bail, can you promise me that?"

"Absolutely. He's a danger to his country. Federal judges won't dream of putting him back on the street."

"That works for me. Now, what about your boy Murfee?"

"We don't tell him yet that we know he's holding out on us. I want to keep that in reserve."

"What else?"

"He's planting a video camera for us in Broyles' office. Should I nix that?"

"No, let it go ahead."

"Why's that?"

"Let's leave the camera in the new office and keep tabs on Broyles' replacement. Something stinks in the U.S. Attorney's office. Let's make sure we've removed all the rotting carcasses before we pull out."

"I won't say anything to Murfee then."

"And keep him in place. The kid is clean and he's getting very valuable in that job. Even more so as he begins to understand his role and the fantastic access it gives him to intelligence. We'll ride that horse into the ground."

"He's a good enough kid," said McGrant. "Even though Friday night he was trying to record me saying I had set him up to spy."

"It happens. They always try that after they've had a few days to consider their own vulnerability."

"It didn't take him long," said McGrant. "Two weeks and bam, he comes at me with one of those spy pens. Spare me, please."

"I know. Amateurs are ruining our world."

Both women laughed. They were old hands at their flavor of counter-espionage and they thrived on knowing they had the upper hand.

"Can you take a trip with me this afternoon?" McGrant asked. "I want to do something."

"I can. What's up?"

"I want to gather up Murfee and have a little chat with him."

"Sure, let's go now."

TEN MINUTES LATER, they managed to locate Thaddeus in the employees' dining room. He was eating alone as it was only 11:30 and the room was deserted. Upon entering, McGrant took up the seat beside him and Ranski settled in across from him. He paused, his tuna salad sandwich halfway to his mouth.

"Uh-oh," he said. "Whatever it is, just please tell me I haven't been terminated."

"No way that's going to happen, Mr. Murfee," McGrant said.

Ranski followed up, "That word, 'terminated.' It means something wholly different a block away from here in the

FBI building than it does here in the U.S. Attorney's building. Funny how that works."

"Thaddeus, you've been here what, three weeks now?"

"Just over two. This is actually the start of my third."

"And you just got paid on Friday?"

"Yes."

"Do you like your job?"

"Yes."

"How would you feel about working as a double agent?"

"What's that?"

"You would be approached by the Chinese. We can make that happen but you don't need to know how. Then you would agree to trade secrets for money. Just like Mr. Broyles."

Thaddeus laid the sandwich aside.

"Are you kidding me? Where do you people come up with this stuff?"

"Your country needs you. Now more than ever."

"You've got the wrong guy. I just want to practice law."

"Sometimes we get called upon to serve our country. You are a patriot aren't you, Mr. Murfee?" said McGrant.

"I don't know about that. I mean if they were on our shores I'd take up a gun and fight. But spying?"

"Here's a news flash," Ranski said with a toss of her head, "they *are* on our shores. The Chinese are here. Half the Middle East is here. The Russians are here. All Americans who hold a unique position in government are being asked to fight back. That's why we're here talking to you, Mr. Murfee."

Thaddeus lifted his sandwich and took another bite. He needed time to think.

Then, "What would I be doing?"

"Spreading disinformation. Giving them bogus data."

"That's it?"

"That's it."

"And in return they give me money?"

"Yes. And it goes into your account in Geneva. They'll be tracking it and it all has to look legitimate."

"Who gets the money when it's all over?"

The agent and the DOJ lawyer looked at each other.

"You," they said in unison.

"Do I get any training? Spy school?"

"There will be some. But mostly you'll be working as a lawyer and meeting them on the side. There won't be any real cloak and dagger. You're needed for this more important role."

"What about my salary? I need at least two-twenty-five to make this work."

"Done," said McGrant. "There will even be a promotion. You'll be taking over Cybercrime's A Team prosecutor job."

Now they had his attention. At long last, a trial lawyer role. This was why he went to law school.

"So you're good with the money and the prosecutor role? Then I'm in. I'll pass along your phony documents and keep the money."

Ranski and McGrant looked at each other. Then they turned and violently shook Thaddeus' hand.

"Welcome aboard," said McGrant. "Come down to my office after lunch. We're ready for you."

"I'll be there. Now if I can finish this tuna in peace, that would be good."

"How is it?"

He paused chewing. "What?"

"The tuna."

"Fishy."

"That's fitting," said McGrant. "The whole world's fishy."

He shrugged and kept chewing. "You beat me to it."

16

Early Tuesday morning, when he was finished checking mail, Thaddeus completed stocking his new office but then shut down his computer, and crept back down to his old office. Busying himself to look like final cleanup before he left the office for good, he suddenly crept up to the door of Broyles' office. There was no one else around in the hallway; he had made sure of that in the last five minutes.

Ever so slowly he twisted the doorknob and peered inside. The office was dark and the curtains drawn. Against one wall were the couch and three opposing chairs, coffee table in the center. Against the wall on his right was the desk facing him, four visitors' chairs and single executive chair--the place where Broyles made the office's policy and selected its victims for prosecution. If Broyles were seated in his chair, the picture of President of the United States would be centered on the wall to his immediate left. It was not a large picture, at most fourteen by twenty inches, and was done in four colors with a tiny engraved tag on the mahogany frame that named the president. Here was Thaddeus' target.

Drawing on a pair of latex gloves, he worked quickly.

The coring tool removed a portion of the subject's lapel, the darkest coloration on the entire photograph. The tool punctured just as Thaddeus had been taught. The piece removed went right into his pocket. Then came the camera. It was inserted from the back side of the photograph until the lens was level with the photo. The lens was tinted and blended well with the president's lapel. It was motion-sensitive and the battery was said to last for up to one month in normal traffic situations. The video was broadcast over a channel that would be received by a card Thaddeus would place in his own computer and then upload to the cloud.

Just as he was securing the camera to the photograph, he heard voices in the hallway beyond his own door. He immediately froze, thought better of it, and hurried back into his office. The voices passed on down the hallway. He waited a full five minutes before again entering Broyles' office and finishing with the installation. He then looked underneath Broyles' desk for the earlier bug he had dropped. Nothing was seen, so he assumed the vacuum got it.

At last his work was completed. Thaddeus crept out of his boss's office and went back to his new office. He opened his own computer, using only a dime as a screwdriver. Inserting the receiver into its empty card slot was a simple task, taking all of four minutes.

Now for the acid test.

Thaddeus returned to Broyles' office and passed back and forth before the presidential visage twice. He counted one to ten out loud. Then he returned to his new office and awaited a text on his cell phone. Moments later, it beeped with a notification of arriving messages: ALL GO.

The camera was in place and producing images and sound.

Thaddeus started loading his final belongings from his old office into a cardboard box. The new office was waiting in the Cybercrime wing and he was ready.

Ready to go to court.

He was sure it was just a matter of time now.

17

The new office wasn't a corner office--only group heads got corner offices--but it was much larger than his old space and much nicer. Fresh paint on the walls, new carpet, clean overhead light covers--it had all been put together to welcome him into his new role. McGrant was keeping up her end of the bargain, which encouraged him and confirmed he had made the right decision. He admired the sign on his outer door. It identified him as the new Cyber-crime A Team lead.

Washington's legal industry had its own daily newspaper, *The Daily Washington Law Reporter*. Thaddeus later that morning picked up a copy on his way back from reading pleadings in the courthouse. There, on the front page, was a file photo of none other than Thad himself, as well as an article about him taking over the A Team on the U.S. Attorney's Cybercrime Task Force. He read it as he walked back to his office. It was thrilling to see his name there; he wondered how many classmates would read the same article. He hoped many would. Most all of them had good feelings for Thaddeus and when he reached his office he was greeted by two new emails from classmates congratulating him. One wondered if there were any openings on his team. He wrote back, stating that team strength was always a secret outside the office, that he couldn't respond. But he suggested she file a resume to the attention of Franklin J. Broyles.

His new secretary arrived from orientation at ten-thirty. She was average height, plump and pretty, with a sailor's vocabulary, he soon found. He had invited her into his office and was discussing his aims for the team and how she could help when she suddenly said, "Let's nail those fucking Chinese. Hate those assholes."

Thaddeus was startled and blinked twice as he composed himself, wondering if he'd heard right.

"Where'd you learn to talk like that," he said. "Were you in the Navy?"

Her name was LaDonna Smits. She smiled broadly.

"I was in the Navy. JAG Corps, paralegal. Came straight out of there to this job. This is my first civilian job since college, Mr. Murfee."

"Please call me Thaddeus when we're alone like this."

"Okay, Thaddeus."

"Now, what we need to do is find some way of prioritizing the cases we've been assigned. It comes to mind that we'll of course want the earlier trial cases arranged by trial dates, but I'm thinking there's another consideration too. We should be thinking in terms of who the defendants are. If there are foreign nations, let's say they get a priority A rating. If they're foreign citizens let's give them a B. If they're U.S., let's call them C's. You see where I'm going with this? We need to prioritize according to threat level, the Chinese threat being an A because they're everywhere we look. They try tens of thousands of incursions into our private and government networks every day. We catch one, we indict them immediately and nail their ass in court."

"I like that, nail their ass in court. You sure you weren't in the Navy?"

He grinned. "Not yet, at least."

"Well, it's great to serve. I encourage any one who's even thinking about it. All my brothers have been in the military. Now we're working on the girls."

"So we will also prioritize by target. If the defendant attacked our government networks, they get a one. If they attacked a private industry network, they get a two. If it was against a citizen, they get a three."

LaDonna turned thoughtful. "Where I was working in financial crimes we also had a category for political referrals. If it was senator or a congressman, the file got marked with a different color. Those matters were controlled more by the group heads because the politicians always had to be stroked."

"Sad but true."

"Fuckers."

"All right. Well, why don't you get settled out there, take the rest of the day, and we'll start reviewing files with our trial team in the morning. Fair enough?"

"Done, boss."

"And please get Donald Zang, Freda Jefferson, Evelyn Sunderburg, and Carlos Estancia in here. We need to have an attorney meeting. Then I'll leave you alone."

Just then, the phone chirped. LaDonna answered and indicated the call was for Thaddeus. He picked up.

"Thaddeus? Melissa McGrant here. Listen, a heads-up. There have been grumblings among the people on your team."

"Don't tell me. They don't like the lateral hire of someone who's never set foot in court."

"How did you know?"

"Right. So how do we handle it?"

"I have explained to them that you're taking over the team and that it's more about your knowledge of computer network technology and system management than about trial expertise. I've asked them to work with you on that."

"But I plan to try the cases at first myself."

"That's fine. They can help with that. I'd just make it clear that you're relying on them to give you the tools you need."

"Fair enough. Will do."

"Call me with any problems."

"Roger that."

Twenty minutes later, he had his trial group gathered around, and they were all offering tips and ideas from prior jobs on how to make the A Team a big success in the U.S.

Attorney's Office. Coffee was slugged down, donuts were imported from elsewhere the in U.S. Attorney's office, OJ was purchased from the MiniMart in the lobby--this was going to take awhile.

"Let's meet again at eight in the morning, Thaddeus finally said. We can begin opening files and making team assignments for prosecution."

"How will work be divvied up?" Freda Jefferson wanted to know.

Thaddeus nodded. "Good question. Initially, I will be first chair on all cases set for trial. If the case is assigned to you, you will be second chair. Once you've helped me through a few cases, you'll start getting first chairs. It's just that I need the experience and I can't think of a better way of getting it. I know Randle Monetti wants more first chairs on the team as fast as we can ramp up."

Monetti was the group leader. Thaddeus would answer directly to him. And he would also report to Melissa McGrant--that hadn't changed, but that was all on the down-low. No one was to know about this private chain of command.

"Mr. Monetti explained to the Team Leads yesterday that our group is going to be the largest group in the U.S. Attorney's office inside of twenty-four months. It's burgeoning, as he put it."

"Who's our biggest customer?" asked Donald Zang, a confident young lawyer from Yale who had been with the office two years. Prior experience included tax prosecutions and organized crime.

"Our biggest customer?"

"Who we have the most files against," Zang smiled.

"The Chinese. Then the Romanians. Then the Russians. Now here's the deal. If the offender has any local presence in the U.S., then we can pick them up and throw them in jail. That's for openers. But if there's no local presence, it's a non-starter."

"We can't prosecute where we don't have jurisdiction over someone."

"Well, we have to look at the statute."

"*The Patriot Act*," said Zang.

"Exactly," Thaddeus agreed.

Freda Jefferson raised her hand and Thaddeus nodded at her. "The *Patriot Act* says that if the crime is committed within the jurisdiction of the United States, we can go after them. Then the Act amended section 1030(e)(2)(b) to specifically include a computer that is used in interstate or foreign commerce, including a computer located outside the U.S. that is used in a manner that affects interstate or foreign commerce or communication of the United States."

"Excellent," Thaddeus said.

"That's broad," Zang added.

"Broad enough we can go after just about anyone on earth," said Ms. Jefferson, a black woman with a headful of braids which she wore short. Thaddeus liked her already, and even more now, with the explication she had just given them.

Another hand went up.

"Carlos?"

"What about domestic crimes? I'm thinking corporate hacking, industrial espionage, that sort of thing?"

"Well, those would be C priority cases, like I've explained. Which doesn't mean they get any less attention, it just means they don't get the first look every day when we come in and switch on our machines."

"FBI liaison?" said Evelyn Sunderburg. "Who has that?"

"Mr. Monetti's arranging all that. It happens upstairs from us."

"So we're just handling prosecutions, none of the sweet talk stuff?"

Thaddeus nodded. "That's what I've been told. We are strictly professional staff, no administrative and no politics, definitely."

"Wonderful," said Sunderburg. "Politics drove us crazy in civil enforcement. I was there for five years. I'm so glad I'm out."

"Well, welcome to the criminal side of the street. We'll work hard and make a name for ourselves and get promotions and great retirement. But not all this first year," Thaddeus laughed.

Just then he was paged by LaDonna.

He stood and walked out into her office.

"Call from a woman who won't give her name."

Thaddeus went into his private office and closed the door.

"Yes?"

"Thaddeus, McGrant. We've just indicted Mr. Broyles. The shit's about to hit the fan. And the FBI intercepted a message from the Chinese mainland. It seems the Chinese have caught onto the article about you in today's legal news. You're the new head of Cybercrime A Team and they want to meet with you."

"How in the hell do you know that?"

There was a pause. "Are you seriously asking me how the CIA staffs and supports these things?"

"No, no, no, I'm not asking that. I'm just impressed. So what do I do?"

"We'd like you to go alone to lunch the rest of this week. See if a contact is made while you're out and about. We're sure you're being followed."

"How do we know that?"

"Eyes, Mr. Murfee. Eyes. Don't ask anymore than that, please."

He sighed. "All right. I'll do lunch today on my own. I'll start with the Can-Am Restaurant downstairs."

"Well, ta-ta. Get back to me when they've made contact. We'll make our plans then."

"Got it."

They said their goodbyes and Thaddeus got back to his group in his conference room.

"One more question came up." It was Freda Jefferson. "What's our division?'

"We're Computer Crime and Intellectual Property Section Criminal Division," Thaddeus replied. "Is that all for now?"

"And my last, last question," Freda said, "What do we do about ten-thirty? That requires the counterespionage peeps to sign off on prosecutions."

"You're referring to section 1030 of the Act?"

"Yes. 1030(a)(1) makes it a felony to access a computer without authorization and obtain certain national security information and then make a willful communication of the information. It's used infrequently, I know, but it's a first priority."

"Well," said Thaddeus, "any steps in investigating or indicting a case under section 1030(a)(1) require the prior approval of the National Security Division of the Department of Justice, through the Counterespionage Section. Please contact them at the two-oh-two number on your handout. We'll have to comply. That's all we can do."

"All right. That answered it."

"Then let's get back to our offices and get busy."

Staff stood and began gathering up papers and laptops. Then they all wandered back to their offices up and down the hallway.

He sat at his desk and checked messages on his computer screen. Nikki called. He thought he might already know what that was about, if news of her father's indictment had hit the streets. He would return that call later.

At 11:40 a.m., he headed downstairs to the Can-Am. He had been there once before, and he had ordered take-out several times. The sandwiches were great; the salads even greater. But this wasn't a time for takeout. He went inside and waited until the hostess showed him to a table. It was a two-seater, against the far wall of the restaurant. It looked out on the sidewalk and a building next door. He thanked her and she plopped a menu down. Thaddeus turned around and sat himself so he was facing the door of the restaurant. He was thinking he might as well make it easy for them just in case they had forgotten what he looked like.

It was Tuesday when this business began. It wasn't until Friday that a contact was made.

He was munching a pastrami sandwich when a bus boy--he thought it was a bus boy, at first--pushing a cart stopped beside him. He was Asian and looked very young.

"Can I sit?" he asked. "Your table is next to do so I'll wait."

While that would ordinarily have been the strangest request of the year, on that particular day it hit Thaddeus like the roof falling in. This was it.

"Sure, have a seat. I'll just be a few more minutes then I've gotta run."

The bus boy looked into his eyes.

"I saw you in the legal newspaper a couple of days ago. Am I right?"

"You did."

"You're Thaddeus Murfee."

"I am. Can I ask your name?"

"My name is David. I don't actually work here."

"You're dressed like you do."

"I represent a client who would like to meet with you."

"And who would that be?"

"A Pacific Rim corporation that wishes to do business in the U.S. In fact, it wishes to do business directly with you, Mr. Murfee."

"That's interesting. But I've already got a job. I don't want to do any other business. Besides, I wouldn't be allowed to even if I wanted."

The young man brushed his hand through the air as if scattering flies. "Don't let that stop you. This is extremely lucrative. I bet your student loans could disappear too."

Thaddeus' face brightened. "How would that work? I owe over two hundred grand."

"Your customer would wave a magic wand and the debt would be gone. Poof!"

"That's interesting. What would this customer want from me?"

"You will have to talk with them about that. Be at the Washington Monument tonight at nine-thirty. The benches on the north side."

"Really? I think I'll pass. Like I said, I'm pretty happy with what I'm doing."

The visitor's face darkened. "Be there, Mr. Murfee. My customer knows about you following our other customer to the Reservoir last week. You were observed spying on our customer. My customer did not like that and would take it very badly if you're not there tonight to meet. My advice? Be there or you're at risk."

"At risk of what?"

But the bus boy was already up and moving his cart toward the kitchen. Thaddeus watched as he suddenly swept off his apron and discarded it and headed for the restaurant's entrance. Then he was gone.

Thaddeus was shaking. They had seen him. They were onto him! McGrant—he was going to need protection. That suddenly rose to the top of his list.

He wouldn't have believed such things happen if he hadn't just witnessed it with his own ears and eyes. But it was what he'd signed up for with McGrant, so he knew better than to not show up at nine-thirty. He decided he would be there and immediately had to stand and tear away to the rest room. Inside, he tossed cold water at his face and suddenly vomited into the sink.

"Fool," he said to his reflection in the mirror.

He'd never felt this scared in his life, not even before the bar exam.

"It's the big leagues, pal," he said to himself.

18

Seven o'clock and Thaddeus was home alone--all roommates were out—and he would ordinarily be enjoying having the apartment to himself. But not tonight. In two hours he was due at the Washington Monument and he would need to leave home in about an hour. His nerves were frayed and every car going past the house was a threat. Or so it felt.

On his desk was his personal laptop, where he was viewing *YouTube* videos of guitar players. *Someday,* he was thinking, *I'm going to learn this stuff.* But he hadn't learned it yet, he thought with dismay, as he picked up his guitar and began chording. But how to make it cry and sing, as Mark Knopfler put it--that was what he wanted to do, playing notes up high on the neck where the pros hang out.

The video ended and that was when he heard the front doorbell, the non-stop ringing. He jumped up and went to the door and pulled it open.

"Nikki, why aren't you at school?"

Actually, he knew why. Her father had been indicted and Thaddeus had called her back when she'd called earlier, but he had only been able to leave a message. So she had come over uninvited and just now was looking desperate.

"You heard about my dad, I'm sure. I'm crushed, Mom's beside herself, and no one knows what to do."

"Come on in. Let me make you some coffee."

"That would be good."

They went into the kitchen and Thaddeus pulled out a kitchen chair for her.

"Sit down, we'll talk," he said.

He served coffee to her and made a second cup for himself. When the Keurig was done steaming, he joined Nikki at the table.

"So. Your father has been indicted. I tried calling you back. Did you get my message?"

She brushed a wisp of hair away from her face and said, "I did, but I was already on my way home and knew I'd be seeing you tonight. We spent the day talking to two different lawyers and got two different opinions about what to do."

"Who did you see? No, wait. I shouldn't ask because it's where I work that's prosecuting your dad. In fact, I should stay out of it altogether."

"No, please. I really need to talk. What if we just talk off the record? Neither of us repeats what we say tonight?"

He looked down at the table top, thinking. Then, "We can try that. But it can't go any further than this room. Agree?"

"Agree. Anyway, we saw Tom Behringer at Scanlon McMann. They're very high profile--"

"I know who they are. I sent them a resume and never heard back when I was looking."

"Then you know all about Tom. He thought my father was probably looking at a long time in jail. He offered my mom very little hope and actually had little useful to say. I came away wondering how Tom Behringer was affected by the fact that my father was U.S. Attorney or what it was exactly that seemed to have him muffled. Anyway, he was nothing like what we were expecting."

"So who was next?"

"Elizabeth L. Robertson at Robertson McNally. Now she's a fireball and we really liked her. But she was adamant the case should go to trial and we should do this and that. I know I'm only pre-law, Thaddeus, but it seemed to me she was painting a pretty rosy picture of what would probably happen if there was a trial. She was pretty confident she could win in court and that my dad would be exonerated. I told my mom that I thought she was overreaching, that maybe she was hard up for a big retainer."

"How much?"

"Tom wanted two-fifty down."

"Two-hundred-and-fifty-thousand?"

"Right. Ms. Robertson wanted five-hundred all at once. She needed the whole amount without giving us some time to get it together."

"When is your dad due in court?"

"Well, they've already had the initial appearance. The judge refused to set bail."

"Why no bail?"

She shrugged. "He said my dad posed a threat to the community. He was afraid my dad would sell more secrets to someone. Something like that."

"What a mess. It sounds just horrible for your whole family."

Tears washed into Nikki's eyes as she sat there. She drew a deep breath and stifled the sobs and then finally let go. She was crying and wiping her eyes when Thaddeus stood and embraced her. Wrapping his arms around her back and pulling her close, he smelled a wonderful fragrance in her hair. Unable to stop himself, he dropped his face to her head and kept it there. Her face turned against his shoulder and then was looking up at him.

"Kiss me, Thaddeus. I need that."

He lowered his head and kissed her fully on the lips. Her lips parted and he tasted her mouth. Suddenly the air was electric and he found himself moving his hands across her back and shoulders then reaching lower and cradling her left cheek in his hand. Which was when it hit him, a moment of lucidity, and he realized what he was doing and understood for the first time the consequences of what he was about to do. He pulled his hands away from the young woman and stood himself upright. He took a step back and held her by the shoulders.

"Nikki, I can't do this. It wouldn't be right."

She wiped a tissue across her eyes.

"Why not?'

"There are certain things I know. And I can't tell you. But I've seen certain things that make me a possible witness against Mr. Broyles."

She suddenly planted her hands on her hips and leaned away from him. "What? You're actually going to testify against my *father*?"

"Now I didn't say that. But certain things have come to my attention and it would be wrong of me to make love to you without you knowing what I know so you can decide if you really want to get mixed up with me. This isn't the best time for you to make that choice. Not until it all comes out and you have all the facts."

"Great! So now you're going to use what I've told you so far? Use it against my dad?"

"No, no, no! You've only told me you saw a couple of lawyers. We haven't discussed anything about the case and we can't. I can't. So I would be taking advantage of you if I had sex with you. You might hate me on down the line and I don't want you to think I used you. Worse, *I* can't do it."

"So you think he's guilty?"

She sat back down and toyed with her coffee cup.

"I didn't say that. I don't even know what the charges are against him. I certainly don't have an opinion whether he's guilty or not."

"So there's hope for him? What about what you know? Is there some way you can get out of using it against him?"

Thaddeus sat down again. He sipped his coffee and closed his eyes, thinking.

"I don't know about getting out of anything. My first inclination, because I like you so much and because I really like Mr. Broyles, is to resign. But even if I do, they could still subpoena me and force me to tell what I know. So resigning doesn't get us anywhere."

There: he had said "us." He had taken sides without really meaning to.

"Doesn't get you anywhere, I mean," he added.

"I just think it's pretty bad that you could come to our house and eat dinner with us and then turn around and tell stuff about my dad that might help send him to prison. I mean, who does that?"

"I know. I hate it, too."

"I'm getting really upset about you, Thaddeus, let me just tell you. I'm getting angry that you would tell someone something about my dad. How did you find out what you found out?"

Thaddeus swallowed hard. This was only going to get worse, he knew. He wished they weren't having this talk, wished they were not part of the Franklin J. Broyles problem.

"I found out because I followed your dad," he said glumly.

"You followed him? Why on earth would you do that?"

He rubbed a hand over his eyes, pushing against his forehead.

"Someone told me to. It was part of my job. Look, I'm sorry.

But when it all happened I hadn't met you yet. I hadn't been to your house. I didn't know how much I was going to like you, Nikki. I didn't know I might even feel stronger than just like. I got really screwed up and I'm sorry."

"Where on earth did you follow him to?"

"Almost to Maryland. Just right across the state line."

"Shit, Thaddeus, how *could* you? He was your *boss*!"

"They told me to. I didn't have any choice."

"Who told you? Was it the FBI?"

"No, it was someone in the office."

She grimaced. "Someone in my dad's office told you to follow my dad? That's beyond the pale. I mean, he gave you a job and then you turn on him?"

Nikki was standing now, pointing a finger at Thaddeus.

"I didn't turn on him. It wasn't personal."

"Ha! That's your excuse, that it wasn't personal. I'm really glad I found out all this about you before I went to bed with you. You were right: I did need to know first. You're a snake, Thaddeus Murfee, and I never want to see you again!"

She turned and stormed to the front door, which she yanked open and then pushed through the outer door. She was standing with it pushed open when she turned and said, "Guys like you just use other people to get ahead. Washington is full of men like you. No--don't say anything, please. Just let me go."

She went on through and the door slammed shut behind

her. Then she was in her car and the lights popped on and she was backing out.

Thaddeus stood at the door long after she had driven out of sight.

He went back into his bedroom and saw his guitar leaning against his desk.

For the first time since he bought the instrument, he suddenly no longer wanted to pick it up and play. Instead, he returned it to its case and clamped the clasps shut one at a time. With his foot he slid it all underneath his bed.

"Damn," he said to himself. "Damn."

He checked his watch.

He was expected at the Washington Monument meeting in seventy minutes. It was time to start moving in that direction.

Nikki wouldn't understand any of this, he thought. *It's better we don't have a thing right now.*

The words made sense but they totally conflicted with his feelings.

He really liked that girl. In fact, now he liked her more than ever.

"Damn."

19

Nikki was out of his life and it really hurt as he picked his way through traffic, arriving at his office later that night. He met with McGrant and Ranski in his own office. Stacked neatly on the conference table were four piles of documents, which Thaddeus would deliver to the Chinese in just over two hours.

Then they launched into just how face-to-face communications would be handled that night.

“If they want U.S. Attorney insider information on prosecution of cyber crimes, what do you do, Thaddeus?" said McGrant.

Thaddeus looked at his notes one last time.

"I'm going to agree to it in Chinese cases but not in other cases. And only if it's an attack on government networks."

"Good," said Ranski. "Now what if it's not cybercrime prosecution information they're after? What if they're after DoD secrets like they were with Frank Broyles?"

He shook his head. "I tell them that I don't have access to those secrets. I tell them that Mr. Broyles had access because he had a man on the inside of the DoD that he had strung out. Someone he could manipulate."

"And what if they ask you to do something else other than secrets?" said McGrant. "What if they ask you to murder someone?"

Thaddeus stifled a laugh. "Right, I'm sure that won't be the case."

"Not so fast," said Ranski. "We've had that request before in another agency."

"What did our guy do?"

"He didn't do anything. We broke off and began prosecution for soliciting murder. A Chinese spy is doing twenty years for that one."

"What are the chances they'll ask me something like that?"

"Very slim," said Ranski. "But it has been known to happen, like I said."

"What else?"

"They might ask you to identify DOJ employees. Or even FBI. No way will we ever do that."

"So basically I'm going to agree only to pass them information on prosecutions of cyber crimes?"

"Right."

"What if they don't want that? What if they want something different?"

Ranski leaned forward at the table. She put her hands on the arm rests and moved her face close to Thaddeus' face. "Again, you have no authority to agree to anything else."

"So just tell them no and walk away?"

McGrant took over. "No, tell them you need to think about it. Then you'll come back and talk to us and we'll make that decision."

"Will you be watching me tonight?"

"Yes. We always have plants around key attractions in Washington."

"So your people are already in place?"

"Twenty-four/seven, Thaddeus. Always. And our people are armed and will intervene in case the other side tries to take you away."

"Will I be wearing a wire?"

"No. They'll pat you down, search you. No wires."

"How will you know if I'm at risk, then?"

"We'll have hidden listening devices nearby. You don't need to worry about that. You'll be safer than you are at home watching *Game of Thrones*."

"I don't watch that. I can't afford HBO."

"Well, whatever. You get my point."

"Yes."

~

JUST BEFORE NINE O'CLOCK, Thaddeus took a cab over to the Washington Monument. They wanted him there early in case the Chinese were early. He paid the cab fare and walked across the grounds to the monument. On the north side he sat down on the curved bench occupying thirty feet of the monument's perimeter. He crossed his legs, leaned back, and tried to appear nonchalant.

Thirty minutes is a long time when you're waiting to meet spies from China, Thaddeus decided. Plus there was a nip in the air, adding to his feeling of being just a little chilled. Or excited--he couldn't tell which.

Sing Di Hoa stepped out of the Metro car at the Smithsonian Station and walked toward the National Mall. He abruptly stopped several times during his walk, keeping to the shadows, and studied the path he was following. Assured no one was following--at least no one he could see--he proceeded to the Washington Monument.

Thaddeus saw the Chinese man approaching from his left. He came upright from his slouch and kept his eyes on the man. The man stopped beside him and took a seat four feet away. For all intents and purposes his attention seemed to be focused on the monument and not on Thaddeus. He produced an iPhone and began snapping pictures of the monument, brightly lit up in a wonderful nighttime light show. Suddenly he spoke to Thaddeus without turning his head and looking at him.

"Mr. Murfee, my friends would like to make you an offer."

"What kind of offer?" Thaddeus replied, keeping his eyes averted as well.

"First remove your coat and unbutton your shirt."

Thaddeus did as he was told. The cold air bit into his skin and he shivered violently.

“Now unbutton your shirt cuffs and pull them up.”

He again complied.

“Now,” Thaddeus said when the man appeared satisfied. “Tell me what your people want.”

"They wish to buy information from you. Information on prosecutions undertaken by your Cybercrimes group."

"Why would I do that? I'm not a traitor."

"No one says you are. But you do sit with the group as its team lead. That is a very important and very powerful position because it gives you knowledge of all prosecutions ongoing. My friends would like to buy information on certain of those prosecutions."

"Would that be prosecutions of China-based operations?"

"It would definitely include those. But there could be others as well."

"And who would be my contact? You?"

"In the beginning, yes. That may change over time. But what would you care? The pay's the same."

"What is the pay?"

"Twenty-five thousand dollars for every internal investigatory file. There are lots of those, I'm sure. You would pay off your student loans in two months. Maybe less."

Thaddeus thought about this for several moments. McGrant and Ranski had promised the money would be his. It was true; he could dump the damn student loans and get on with his life. Maybe buy a condo. Maybe even a condo in Georgetown. Now that would be something. His thoughts roamed on, considering what the money could mean to him. But then the man said something that burst the thought bubble.

"We would also want to buy information on certain members of the U.S. Attorney's Office. Certain personnel files."

"Why?"

"We might wish to gain leverage with those certain people."

"You mean you wish to get something on people and blackmail them?"

The man looked over from his picture-taking. It was the first time their eyes met.

"Now that's characterizing our work as something base. It's not. We just want to offer similar opportunities to others in your office who might be amenable to enriching themselves."

"Mister," said Thaddeus, "you just said the same thing twice but with different words. You're telling me you might want to blackmail my colleagues. That is a definite no. That is something I wouldn't do, give you information on colleagues."

The man smacked his lips. "That would have to be part of our arrangement, Mr. Murfee."

"Then you've got the wrong guy."

A silence settled over the two men. Thaddeus had just

broken ranks; his handlers were going to be furious if he didn't strike a deal.

"I'm in, if all I'm selling is investigatory files. I'm not in if you want information about people in my office. I won't do that."

"Then we don't have anything else to talk about, Mr. Murfee. The personnel information is part of our bargain."

"I wouldn't have access to such data anyway."

"You would figure out how. We would help you."

"Can't do it, mister. Sorry."

"Your loss, Mr. Murfee."

With that, Hoa got up and began walking away. Thaddeus had the strong sense that he had just blown it up. He had been commissioned to make contact and strike a deal. But he had refused and now he was in no hurry to explain what just happened to McGrant, who most likely had just listened to everything that was said.

And he was right. She was furious. Back at the U.S. Attorney's office she was waiting for him in his office. When he walked in, he knew it wasn't going to be good: McGrant was seated in his chair behind his desk.

"I blew it. I just couldn't agree."

"You had no permission to blow it. We would have provided disinformation on our employees. It meant nothing, Thaddeus."

Agent Ranski came breezing in then and took a seat next to Thaddeus. She was shaking her head and exhaling sharply before she spoke.

"Well your spying career just came to a screeching halt. You really let us down, Murfee. We're going to terminate you."

Thaddeus looked up at McGrant, who only nodded.

"You're done here, Thaddeus. Clean out your desk. You'll receive two weeks' severance."

He drew a deep breath. McGrant and Ranski left him to clear out and leave.

Sitting back in his chair, he knew what he had to do. He had known it all along.

He dialed Nikki's number.

"Hello?"

"Thaddeus here, Nikki. Has your father retained a lawyer yet?"

"No, why?"

"Because he has one now."

"Who?"

"Thaddeus Murfee."

20

Aloysius M. Barnaby looked up from the motion and glared down at Thaddeus. Thaddeus hadn't been around enough to know that here sat one of the most inappropriately judgmental judges in the D.C. circuit. It wasn't that his actual judging was faulty. Rather, his personal judgments about defendants and their lawyers was demeaning and ethically questionable.

That day in January Judge Barnaby had sitting before him Thaddeus and Franklin J. Broyles, on one side, and Assistant U.S. Attorney Oliver Anderson on the prosecution side. Thaddeus--from his work at the U.S. Attorney's office--knew Oliver as "Ollie" and knew the prosecutor as someone who loathed criminal defendants. Ollie's having his ex-boss, Franklin Broyles, in his gunsights was a pleasure and an unexpected joy because it satisfied Ollie's bloodlust and need to be seen around town as a high-profile litigator. In short, he was loving seeing Broyles demeaned by Judge Barnaby and watching Thaddeus knocked to the ground again and again. That Thaddeus kept getting right back up and dusting himself off and plunging ahead with his defense of Broyles was off-putting, but Anderson knew it would eventually wear the young lawyer down to the point of total intimidation. Then maybe he would sit the hell down and keep his eager mouth shut.

It was nine-thirty a.m. The jury was all picked--six men and six women, seven blacks and five whites. Press was crowding the courtroom and, with the boldness of people used to interrupting others, there was an unwelcome buzz in the courtroom as reporters whispered back and forth. TV crews noisily broadcast the proceedings nationwide. It was a headline case. The anchors and their henchmen were leaving no stone unturned. It wasn't every day that a sitting U.S. Attorney was arrested and charged with selling state secrets. The penalty could be death because the federal government always sought the death penalty for treason and espionage and so the air inside the courtroom was electric. Every word counted and the audience was missing none of it.

At long last the judge, having read Thaddeus' motion to dismiss the charges against his client, was visibly unimpressed. His round face glowed red and he tugged repeatedly at his necktie as if trying to inhale more air.

"Mr. Murfee," he finally said, laying the motion aside, "your motion is all over the road."

Thaddeus stood. "Sir?" he replied, not knowing how else to respond.

"Your pleading is confused and, I believe, purposely misleading. You argue that I should dismiss the government's case because Mr. Broyles was in fact a double-agent. I assume you can prove this?"

"We can, Your Honor. We will call--"

The judge instantly raised his hand and pointed a finger at Thaddeus.

"Please, sir, it's not who you call and what they say, it's whether you can convince *me*, at this time and place, that your client has been wrongly accused. There is no evidence before me and to ask that I dismiss these charges without evidence is--well, it's preposterous. Let me ask you sir, have you ever even appeared in federal court before?"

"No, Your Honor," Thaddeus said in his best voice. He was determined to sound strong and unflinching. He had no idea if he sounded strong and unflinching. Worse, he had no idea if he even was those things. "It's my first time in the barrel," he had told Nikki that morning. "Say a prayer."

The judge's eyes narrowed.

"Well, let's dig a little deeper. Have you ever appeared in any court before?"

"No, Your Honor."

"Well, Mr. Murfee, my inclination is to delay the beginning of these proceedings in order to allow your client to secure experienced trial counsel. It is unheard of for a first-time lawyer to defend a capital crime. Your client is facing the death penalty and, quite frankly, sir, I don't believe you have what it takes to adequately defend him."

"Your Honor, it might surprise you to know this, but both my client and I agree with what you just said. My client's family agrees with what you just said. And they have tried to secure more experienced counsel for their loved one."

"Well?"

"The truth is, no attorney will touch this case."

"Why is that, Mr. Murfee?"

"We believe it's because every lawyer in this town relies on the government for their income in some way or other. No one wants to give up their hold on the government in order to defend a man accused of treason. It's a very unpopular crime, Your Honor."

Judge Barnaby smirked and put his hands together, moving them as if washing.

"Well, Mr. Murfee, let me just say this. I have never tried a treason case either. Ordinarily there's a plea and someone goes to jail for a very long time. But in this case the new U.S. Attorney has taken the position that there will be no plea. In papers he has filed with the court he has made it clear that he is seeking the death penalty. So it's a first time for me; however, unlike you, I have been to court lots of times and I'm immensely competent to preside over this case. You, however, have yet to prove your competence. So here's what I'm going to do. I'm going to direct the clerk to call Homer X. Matheson and get him in court immediately. Do you know who Mr. Matheson is, Mr. Murfee?"

Thaddeus shrugged. "Only that he's a lawyer. I've heard the name."

"Mr. Matheson is the greatest criminal lawyer we've ever had in Washington. He's defended senators, congressmen, politicians, military personnel, and just about everything else. He is going to come here and assist you in the trial of this case. And do you know why I'm doing this, Mr. Murfee?"

"Because you're afraid of a claim on appeal that my client's counsel was ineffective? That I blew it?"

"Bingo! I am going to quell any such argument by having you mentored in my courtroom, Mr. Murfee. That way we might avoid some of the ridiculously stupid mistakes and errors in judgment that young lawyers like you are prone to make. Are you following me, Mr. Murfee?"

"I am hearing what you say, Your Honor. But I think you'll find my defense lacking the ridiculously stupid mistakes and errors in judgment you're used to. In fact, I project that by the time this case is over and I have obtained a verdict of acquittal you're going to want to shake my hand and congratulate me on a job well done."

The courtroom fell deathly silent. A line had been crossed by the young lawyer and everyone there knew it. Judge Barnaby's reputation was known far and wide among the Washington criminal bar. The kid was doomed; any other practitioner would have said. He had just slit his own throat.

"Mr. Murfee, that is very naive. Which only further confirms your lack of experience."

Just then the clerk returned to the courtroom and took up her position at the side of the judge's throne. She looked up at the judge and nodded.

"He's on his way over, Your Honor," the clerk said meekly.

"Very well. Mr. Murfee, I'm going to take a thirty-minute recess. You are ordered to meet with Mr. Matheson during our recess and prepare your defense. We stand in recess."

21

Four months before trial began, Thaddeus had met with Franklin Broyles. Broyles was still in jail; they met in an attorney conference room on the first floor, on the east side of the jail in southeast D.C. It was a bare room furnished with a five-by-five metal table bolted to the cement floor, with a metal chair on each side. The chairs were also bolted to the floor. Presumably, Thaddeus reasoned, so a chair couldn't be used to make a break for it. Broyles was brought by two guards to the meeting. He was wearing an orange jumpsuit that said in stenciled letters across the back CDF (Central Detention Facility) and wearing flip-flops though the interior of the building was air conditioned and uncomfortably cold.

"Can you get me some wool socks?" was the first thing Broyles asked him, which established Thaddeus in the environment in which Broyles existed. He had never seen the inside of a jail before. Fear and claustrophobia were his immediate visceral response to what he saw there.

"I can try to get you socks," he said to Broyles.

"You are my lawyer, evidently," said the ex-U.S. Attorney. "Jeannette said last night on the phone that no one else would touch the case. Why do you think they won't, Thaddeus?"

"Fear, I imagine. No one wants to taunt the government with an aggressive defense of an indicted U.S. Attorney. Every lawyer in D.C. gets government money some way or another. No one will risk losing that."

"Then I'm in hell. Look, I appreciate you stepping up for me, but you are really useless. You have no experience, have never attended even a hearing in a federal court, know nothing about jury selection and probably even less about the crime of treason. I don't mean to make you feel bad, but there you are. You're basically helpless, which makes me hopeless. The trouble is, I have nowhere else to turn except to defend myself. Which never works, so I'm left with you. You're hired, which scares the living hell out of me.

"Me too."

" But one thing, Thaddeus: we'll go down together. I won't desert you if you'll make the same promise to me."

"I promise," said the young lawyer. "I'll be with you to the bitter end. Or the happy miracle, should Providence intervene."

Broyles had hung his head at that point, his chin on his chest, and wrung his hands together in total frustration.

"One thing, Mr. Broyles--"

"Frank. We're on first names now, Thaddeus."

"All right--Frank. One thing, are you guilty of treason?"

Broyles shook his head violently. "No, not at all."

"How can you say that? I personally witnessed you passing a briefcase to a stranger at the reservoir."

"I was a double agent, Thaddeus."

"I don't know for certain what that means."

"I was working for the government of the United States while appearing to be a thief of government secrets who was selling them to the Chinese."

Thaddeus was stunned. He sat several minutes without saying anything while Broyles repeatedly flexed his hands. The man was obviously in psychic pain. He drew Thaddeus in with his helplessness. The young lawyer's heart went out to the guy. He committed himself to doing whatever it took to have him found not guilty.

"How do we prove you were a double agent?"

"There's proof on the computers at the U.S. Attorney's office. I know it's there, hidden on our servers."

"You know it's there?"

Broyles smiled for the first time. "I put it there myself. On our servers. They'll never find it. I had help from a man who works at Geek Squad. He told me how to hide it."

"Why would you do that?"

"I didn't trust the government. It is a tradition among double agents to hide artifacts that can prove their innocence. I was only protecting myself in case the eagle one day turned on me. Now it has, but the evidence which can exonerate me is in there. Now if we can only figure out how to access it. You see, my passwords and back doors into the data have all been removed. The data might as well be on the moon for all the good it does me here today. I'm guilty without it. There's a second set of records that I do have. They would be banking records."

"Wait. Why would the government come after you? That's what I don't understand."

"Because I came into secrets about the Hong Kong bank known as HSBC. Those are the banking records. I came into possession of a hundred thousand names of U.S. Citizens who kept numbered accounts there in order to avoid paying taxes. Thousands of politicians, bankers, and lobbyists in Washington were among those names. This would include people in the DOJ."

"How are you sure?"

"How do I know DOJ officials are hiding money offshore? I know because I looked. The data was contained in a database that made mining very simple. Because I had it, and because the DOJ became aware of what I had, the government turned on me. They came after me in order to shut me up."

"Are you able to access the banking records?"

Broyles had smiled broadly at that point. "I am."

"How?"

"It's all on the hard drive of Nikki's computer. The laptop she keeps at school. I put it there."

"Oh my God. Does that put her at risk?"

"I would never put my daughter at risk. No, no one has any

idea it's stored there. I made sure of that before I presented her with the computer as a Christmas present last year. The database is disguised as a system file by using a system extension. Pretty damn clever, aren't I?"

"Does the government know you have them?"

"They think that by cutting me off from their servers they have secured them from me. They have no idea I have the banking records apart from there."

"So how do we use these records?"

"We don't. I do."

"How?"

"Imagine how much these account holders would be willing to pay me in return for my guaranteeing that I would dump their data?"

"Unbelievable. So you would use the banking records to extort money from the owners?"

"I don't look at it quite like that, Thaddeus. The money is money they've stolen from the government by not paying it out in taxes. I'm just my own version of Robin Hood."

"And the records that prove you were working for the government—do you have those hidden on her computer too?"

"No, those were all newer. I never had a chance to place them outside the government servers. Damn that luck!"

They had gone on from there for another hour, talking into the late afternoon about the defense against the charge of treason and espionage. It came out that Broyles had been given phony Department of Defense documents to pass to the Chinese. In return he got the banking records. In the milieu of traitors and spies, it was called disinformation, what Broyles turned over. But the banking records from HSBC bank that Broyles was given in exchange were real.

The two men ended the visit with the first glimmer of hope since the world came crashing down. Vows of loyalty were made again and they broke off at four-thirty on a boiling hot August afternoon.

Thaddeus had come away wondering how on earth they would ever access the government computers and retrieve the proof that Broyles was working for the government. That was going to be the true test.

For now, he didn't possess that answer. Like Broyles, he only had hopes.

He knew he would have to do better. Hope never won a criminal trial.

Only evidence could do that.

The kind that was stored on the government's computers.

22

Thaddeus met Homer X. Matheson for the first time in the hallway outside Judge Barnaby's courtroom. There were twenty minutes remaining in the thirty-minute recess when they disappeared into the attorney conference room. Twenty minutes to decide on a defense and plan their cross-examination of FBI agent Naomi Ranski.

Ranski was the agent who, along with McGrant, had approached Thaddeus in the cafeteria at the U.S. Attorney's Office and solicited his help in feeding disinformation to the Chinese. She would be called to provide the government's twenty-thousand-foot view of the case. Prosecutors always lead off with the lead investigator in criminal cases, and that's how it would happen with the Franklin Broyles prosecution.

Matheson was black with the physique of a hundred-meter dash man. His face was the face of a much younger man than his actual fifty years. Black frame glasses gave him a studious look and, Thaddeus quickly learned, the look was a valid one. Because here was a man who knew criminal law forward and backward, a man who'd tried over a hundred criminal cases to verdict in the D.C. federal court and was lead appellate counsel on an equal number. He had large hands which moved frequently as he spoke, as did his very expressive face. He cited case law to Thaddeus and tested him on the kinds of evidentiary objections he could expect to be making as the trial progressed. When their time was up, Thaddeus knew he had just been handed a dozen years of experience in twenty minutes. It was a welcome relief just knowing Matheson was there for questions.

When court resumed, FBI Agent Naomi Ranski was called to the witness stand and sworn. She then proceeded to describe her role in the Broyles case. As it turned out, she was the lead FBI agent on the investigation of Franklin J. Broyles. It had been ongoing for three years.

Broyles had been wire-tapped and a highlight recording of his limited telephone discussions with the Chinese was played for the jury. Thaddeus studied the jurors' face as the recording rocked along; he was dismayed to see their expressions go from neutral to troubled to angry, frowning citizens whose government had been compromised. They were clearly unhappy and angry when the recording switched off.

Next came over two hundred photos of Broyles meeting with the Chinese. At the reservoir, in restaurants, at D.C. tourist locations and National Mall attractions--they were never-ending, Broyles' meetings with the Chinese. Thaddeus' heart fell as he studied the photos, but he told himself over and over that his client was a double agent and of course he would meet with spies.

Then came the numbered accounts, Hong Kong flavor and

Swiss flavor. The IRS had its methods; the banking records were obtained and came into evidence providing damning proof of Broyles' receipt of huge sums of money from unexplained sources. One thing the prosecution made clear: the money Broyles' stashed sure as hell wasn't from his paycheck.

Finally, the prosecutor asked Ranski why she had let the spying go on so long.

"We were providing him with disinformation. It took the Chinese three years to figure out what we were feeding them was bogus."

"Did Broyles know it was bogus?"

"Broyles never knew what he was passing along," Ranski said. "He only gave a hoot about the money he was getting."

"Was he receiving cash?"

"Almost never. They would make deposits into his HSBC account in Hong Kong. Usually within the first twenty-four hours after he had handed them another briefcase stuffed with documents."

"Has Broyles made any statements to anyone since his arrest?"

"Not that I know of. My team has been on him twenty-four/seven since this all began three years ago. He is very well-known around our Washington office."

"That is all."

The judge peered down at Thaddeus. "Counsel, you may cross-examine."

Thaddeus stood and moved to the lectern. His heart was pounding so hard he feared the jury might see the pulse in his throat.

"Ms. Ranski, did you ever recruit me to cooperate with the Chinese?"

"No. I hardly know who you are."

"You don't remember coming to the cafeteria in my building and soliciting me to pass information to the Chinese?"

"Not at all," she scoffed. "I haven't even spoken with you before right now."

"You don't recall a meeting of you, me, and Melissa McGrant?"

"Objection, Your Honor," the Assistant U.S. Attorney cried. "This has been asked and answered three times now."

Judge Barnaby gave Thaddeus an icy look. "Counsel, move it along. We don't want to bore our jury."

Thaddeus felt a stab of embarrassment. Judge Barnaby's claws had raked him, just like he was known to do. He winced and smiled at the Judge, his hands trembling. "Your Honor, I am positive the truth never grows old with juries."

"Counsel, that's out of line. Your commentary is inappropriate and if it happens again there will be sanctions, sir."

"Yes, Your Honor."

Thaddeus heard Matheson whisper sharply at him. "Thaddeus!"

He turned and joined the older lawyer at counsel table, lowering his head to listen.

"Don't cross this bastard, Thaddeus!" Matheson whispered. "He can make your trial a living hell if you do it again."

Thaddeus nodded and returned to the lectern.

"Agent Ranski, isn't it true you solicited Mr. Broyles to spy for you?"

"Not true."

"You didn't tell him he would be passing along disinformation and that he could keep the money he received in return?"

"Never."

"You didn't convince him how helpful he would be to his country if he went undercover?"

"I--I--"

"Counsel!" barked Judge Barnaby. "What did I just tell you about asking the same questions multiple times?"

Thaddeus turned to respond and saw the judge was leaning forward on his elbows, his face red with rage. Thaddeus thought better than to fight back.

"Sorry, Judge. I'm still pretty green at trials. I'm not doing it to ignore what you said."

"Very well. Move it along, then," the Judge said with no small disgust. It was very clear how he felt toward the young lawyer and, by extension, his client.

"Ms. Ranski," Thaddeus continued, "let's talk about the true nature of Frank Broyles' work with you. Isn't it a fact that he was actually a double agent?"

She dodged. "What does that mean, 'double agent?'"

Thaddeus smiled. "An agent who is actually working for the government but makes it look like he's selling government secrets. Wasn't that the true nature of what the FBI and Mr. Broyles were doing?"

"No, it was not."

"What if he says it was?"

"He'd be lying. It simply wasn't true."

"Isn't it true that while he was working for you he came into possession of foreign bank records that had the potential to send many politicians and elected officials to jail?"

"No, that's not true."

"Are you familiar with HSBC bank out of Hong Kong?"

"Yes, I've heard of them."

"Did Frank Broyles ever come into possession of HSBC account records that you knew of?"

"Not that I knew of."

Thaddeus looked through his notes. The judge sighed impatiently as he did so. Then again.

Finally, Judge Barnaby said, "Counsel were you finished with your cross-examination?"

"No, Your Honor. I'm just checking my notes."

"Well let's move it along. The jury is impatient and I am too."

It was just the wrong thing to say to Thaddeus right then because he was frustrated, with, first of all, the agent's lies, and, second of all, his notes were almost indecipherable and he knew his examination of the witness was incomplete but couldn't find the other notes to guide him. So he reacted.

"Judge Barnaby, I don't believe the jury feels impatient. I believe they know I'm new at this and they're giving me the chance to do this right."

Judge Barnaby reacted solemnly. "The bailiff will take the jury to the jury room."

The bailiff did as he was told. Then, when the courtroom was clear of jurors, Judge Barnaby exploded.

"Mr. Murfee! Those comments just cost you a night in jail."

Thaddeus turned to face the man.

"I don't get it, Your Honor. I thought this proceeding was a search for the truth. You have turned it into a search for the fastest way to move things along even though it might hurt my client. This is wrong, wrong, wrong!"

Judge Barnaby didn't reply. He checked his watch. It was just before noon. Soon the jury would head out to lunch and they wouldn't take up again until 1:30. So he made his decision.

"The marshals will take Mr. Murfee and place him in the U.S. Marshall's holding cell. When the court recesses for the day the marshals will return him to jail until nine o'clock tomorrow morning when we take up again. You, sir," he was pointing down at Thaddeus now, his white finger waggling, "you are in contempt. You will serve a night in jail for it. Do it again and you'll serve twenty-four hours in jail. A third time and you're buying yourself a week. Do you understand all this?"

"Of course I do, judge. I didn't just fall off the turnip wagon."

"Two nights and counting. Anything else, Mr. Murfee?"

At just that moment, Homer Matheson approached Thaddeus from behind, whispered in his ear, and took him by the elbow and returned him to counsel table.

"Your Honor," said Matheson. "Mr. Murfee accepts the court's correction and makes his apology."

"Marshal Studea, please remove Mr. Murfee now. Return him to the courtroom at one-thirty. We're in recess."

He pounded his gavel and Thaddeus was immediately being guided from the courtroom in the strong grip of Marshal Studea.

"I'll be right over, Thaddeus," Matheson called to him. "Let me finish up with Mr. Broyles here and we'll talk."

"That's fine, Homer," said Thaddeus as he was being steered through the doors. "I enjoy being alone. This will be a rest cure for me."

23

He'd never been in jail before.

But he wasn't scared.

Matheson arrived just after Thaddeus was booked. He met with the young lawyer for about an hour. Did Thaddeus have proof of his claim that Broyles was a double agent? Thaddeus said Broyles had proof but he was locked up and had no access. Matheson wanted to know the location of the proof. Thaddeus said Broyles had told him it was on the U.S. Attorney's network servers. Both men thought about this for several minutes.

"How do we get to it?" Matheson asked.

"Steal it," Thaddeus replied. It was blunt and it was direct and it was the truth. The way Broyles had explained it to him, he no longer had access. The double agent proof was out of their reach.

"Let me think about this," Matheson finally said as he was leaving. "There must be some way."

After court got underway at 1:30, the Assistant U.S. Attorney spent the afternoon going back over Agent Ranski's testimony. Ollie Anderson wanted to be certain there was nothing left unanswered. Thaddeus was given a chance for re-cross examination, which he kept going until they recessed at five o'clock.

The marshals transported him to jail and left without a word. No one wanted to say anything that might somehow get back to the judge, not even the usually friendly marshals.

Which left Thaddeus alone with his cellmates. He took a look around at the faces.

Everyone there looked lost and alone. They found out he was a lawyer and one by one pleaded their case to him. Everyone was innocent, of course. Criminal lawyers know that a guilty man has never gone to jail and a guilty man has never been locked away in prison. There is only unproven innocence.

Thaddeus listened but there was nothing he could offer. He was in jail just like them and besides, even if he weren't, he still had a trial underway. He couldn't offer help to any of them. Just a patient ear.

Which was enough to get him through the night without incident.

He awoke the next morning after spending the night shivering on a thin mattress.

It was a different feeling in his gut than the day before. He was angry. He was angry and he was determined he wouldn't back down from some bully in a black robe.

He might spend a week in jail, maybe more, but he was going to defend Frank Broyles for all he was worth.

He owed it to Frank.

24

The second morning of trial, Thaddeus renewed Broyles' motion for bail. It infuriated Judge Barnaby: the very idea that Thaddeus would ask for a second hearing on a motion once denied.

They were sitting in the judge's chambers and Thaddeus was explaining why he wanted the conference.

"Your Honor--are we on the record?"

"Yes," said the judge.

"It is making it very difficult to defend my client adequately with him locked away in a jail cell. There are certain preparations we must make for his adequate defense that require his personal assistance. I'm not at liberty to say what these things are, but I avow to the court that they are real and pressing."

"Counsel, your avowal means nothing to the court. I don't know you and I don't know whether you're telling the truth or not and frankly don't give a damn. Mr. Broyles stays in jail because he still threatens the United States if he is allowed out."

"What threat would that be again?" Thaddeus asked.

The judge turned red. "We've been over this Mr. Murfee. But for the record, it is the court's concern that if he is admitted to bail he will pass additional secrets to a foreign power. He's already done that and he might do it again. I'm unwilling to take that risk."

"Your Honor," Thaddeus persisted, "I move that you continue the trial for two weeks so that I can file an emergency appeal. I don't think your reasoning is sound and I believe the appellate court will overturn your refusal for bail. Can I be any clearer? We need this continuance, Your Honor. No one is prejudiced by a two week stay. If anyone would be it would be the defendant and the defendant waives any such prejudice. Please, Judge, let me help my client."

Judge Barnaby's white eyebrows shot up. "Help your client? I doubt that's going to happen at all in this trial, Mr. Murfee. Not from what I've seen out of you thus far. It was a mistake allowing you to defend Mr. Broyles. A mistake I already regret. But we're underway now and my hands are tied. I can't prevent you from continuing although Mr. Broyles--" speaking now to Broyles himself, "--certainly should. Mr. Broyles you might want to seriously reconsider your decision to have Mr. Murfee defend you. It's not going well."

"Thank you, Judge," said Broyles. "I don't want anyone else. Mr. Murfee has plans to walk me out of here a free man and I trust that."

Judge Barnaby broke into laughter. "A free man, you say? Very doubtful, Frank. Very doubtful."

"Two weeks, Judge, that's all I'm asking," Thaddeus said again. "But you're not going to allow it because you've already found my client guilty of passing secrets to the Chinese. Am I wrong, here, Judge?"

"Mr. Murfee, if I have to gag you to put an end to your ranting and raving at me, sir, I will do just that. While I can't keep you in jail all day just now, I sure as hell can and will when this trial is over. For the record, no finding of guilt on any issue in this case has been made by the court. My mind is completely unbiased right now."

Thaddeus pushed. "Then how can you keep Mr. Broyles in jail? You're assuming he's a risk. And assumptions are based on beliefs. You must believe he's a threat in order to assume he's a risk. So you see, Judge Barnaby, you have made a finding of guilt regardless of what you say."

At this point, Homer Matheson seized Thaddeus' upper arm. He bodily lifted him out of his chair and removed him from Judge Barnaby's chambers. He slammed the door behind them, virtually ending the court session that wasn't yet officially ended.

"Goddamn it, Murfee! Shut the hell up, man! Get hold of yourself. That man is going to put you in prison if you keep after him like that!"

Thaddeus didn't answer. He pushed on down the hallway toward the elevators. He immediately caught a descending elevator car and jumped inside. The doors closed behind him and he rode with two other people down to the lobby, clenching his eyes shut the entire way.

Meanwhile, Matheson crept back into the judge's chambers and bowed and scraped until he had managed to convince the judge to end the session without leveling contempt sanctions and more jail time against Thaddeus. Judge Barnaby was implacable in his resolve, however, to punish Thaddeus. He told Matheson that Thaddeus could very possibly spend the rest of the year in jail after the trial ended. Matheson started to argue, but they were off the record and he feared the judge would even bring charges against him, Matheson. So Matheson simply thanked the judge and rushed from the office. He inhaled a huge breath when he was outside the judge's door. What the hell was wrong with Murfee? he asked himself. The kid was totally out of control. How could he make him understand that lawyers didn't act that way with judges?

Outside on the sidewalk, Thaddeus walked up to the nearest streetlight and back to the courthouse three times. He was sucking in oxygen and fighting to calm himself. *You're going to have to learn how to keep that anger down,* he told himself. *Judges have all power and they believe they are all-seeing. They can put you in jail and there's nothing anyone can do about it because judges have the final say-so. Get angry, get mad, drink yourself silly if you need to, but don't ever, ever expose your soul to a judge like that again. Never.*

He swore to himself, right then and there, that he would take his own advice. In fact, it was beginning to dawn on him that he was going at it all wrong. He didn't need to outshout judges and rail against them. No, he needed to outsmart them. That's why he had graduated third in his class, because he had outworked and outsmarted ninety-seven other very bright people who had managed to get themselves admitted to law school three years ago. That was saying something. He turned and went back inside the building, feeling more confident by the moment that he was onto something. He was going to outsmart the folks in the black robes. If he didn't, he would languish in jail and that helped exactly no one. Least of all clients like Frank Broyles.

Now, he would start the day over. The United States was going to call to the stand its second FBI agent. He needed to be clear-headed for that.

Punching the UP button just once and resisting the compulsion that would have him push it over and over obsessively, he waited calmly for the car to arrive.

Then he was back upstairs and just taking his seat as Judge Barnaby ascended to his place on high.

He didn't go there; he didn't call it a throne.

Even though Barnaby sat it like one.

25

Woodrow T. Chin just made the FBI cutoff height at the lower end of the scale for Special Agents. As such he was what some might call "short," but he was powerfully built--even ape-like--a world class Karate black belt with a glass case full of gold cups and blue ribbons. The Chinese agent was without any sun color and he wore his black hair in a crewcut, lending him the look of a math geek straight out of UCLA. Which he was, hailing from Orange County, hence his conservative mindset and instant willingness to sign on with the FBI straight out of law school in order to help protect the Constitution and the American way of life.

Agent Chin was the first witness to take the stand the second morning of trial. Thaddeus looked him over, deciding where he was going to find a hole in the man's story based on who the man appeared to be. As the direct exam proceeded, then Thaddeus' inquiry shifted from the man's appearance to the man's context--what he had to say about his investigation and role in the investigation of

Franklin J. Broyles. From this he would come to know where to chip away. The young lawyer was learning as he went.

Agent Chin testified he had worked hand-in-glove with Agent Ranski in investigating Broyles. He had been recruited by the Chinese to acquire U.S. Intelligence papers and sell them, according to Chin. He had performed admirably--for a traitor and an enemy of America. Was he possibly working as a counter-agent--a double agent as suggested by defense counsel?

No, Chin testified vehemently, no such thing. He was a traitor and had been from the very start. He had been arrested only when his usefulness to the government dried up. But what about the security secrets he sold to the Chinese? Wasn't that a terribly dangerous criminal act? The security secrets were all disinformation, Chin said with the hint of a smile. Secrets and tales and data concocted to mislead the Chinese into thinking it was legitimate, reliable, and actionable intelligence China could draw from to improve its own security and offensive capabilities.

Then it was Thaddeus' turn to cross-examine. He made his way up to the lectern after a fifteen-minute mid-morning rest and restroom break.

"Now," he said to Chin in a friendly voice, "Mr. Chin, your ethnicity is Chinese?"

"Yes."

"But you were born in the U.S.A.?"

"Every bit as American as you, Mr. Murfee."

"Thank you. I appreciate that, and your nationality and patriotism were never disputed, sir."

Chin nodded without smiling.

"But what I don't understand--and what maybe the jury is also not understanding--is why a sitting United States Attorney would turn sour. Why would a loyal American suddenly agree to turn bottom-up and start betraying his country? Can you explain how that happened in this case? I mean, your whole case depends on the jury believing your story that the Chinese turned the guy from a patriot to a traitor. How did this work, exactly?"

Chin looked over at the jury.

"The power of money should never be underestimated. Its allure is a story as old as the shiny stones that were first exchanged by our progenitors who lived in caves and marveled at fire. Acquisition is the national pastime in the United States, not baseball. The defendant was no different from any other American whose soul is defined by bank balances. That's your client, Mr. Murfee. We didn't make him that way; we only tapped into it."

"So he was by nature a thief? Is that it?"

"Yes."

"But this never showed up anyplace in his entire life before. He has never been accused of cheating on law school or even college examinations. He has never floated a bad check, never knocked a little old lady down and made off with her purse, never cheated on his taxes. The tax thing is even vetted by the FBI before a U.S. Attorney gets sworn in. Your own employer vouched for his honesty. Yet here you are, swearing before the jury that Chinese agents were able to inoculate him against his own honest character and produce a traitor willing to do their will for a dollar. Is that it?"

"Nice speech, counsel," Chin replied with the hint of a smile. "Did you really want me to take a shot at that?"

Thaddeus managed to exude frustration. "Of course. That's why I asked the question, sir."

"In answer to your speech, yes. The Chinese were able to inoculate him against his honest character, as you so eloquently put it. They turned him, in agent-speak."

"Who of the Chinese first approached Mr. Broyles?"

“A man whose name doesn’t matter. A Chinese national.”

“Now, how do you know this?”

“I had penetrated their cell. I was a double-agent.”

“When was he first approached by this no-name man?”

“Three years ago. At a state function in Washington."

"Tell us what happened at that function."

"He was with his wife that evening. It was at an orchestral performance of some kind. At intermission he excused himself and went to obtain a drink for his beautiful wife and himself. As he was turning away from the cash bar, two wineglasses in hand, I introduced myself to him."

"What, as Agent Chin of the FBI?"

"Not at all. Under an assumed name. Mr. No-Name was with me. Talk then progressed. We moved over against the wall beside a twisting staircase. In its shadow we proceeded to talk for a good ten minutes until the lights blinked, signaling the start of the second half of the show. He gave me his private phone number and agreed that I could call him. After that, we met three times more, always in broad daylight at some location or other either at or within a stone's throw of the National Mall."

"What was discussed at those meetings?"

"At first we talked politics. Then government rights and wrongs. He was very upset with the U.S. Incursions into Iraq and Libya and Afghanistan. Thought the U.S. was far exceeding the War Powers clause of the Constitution. He thought the government was out of control, which is where I found my opening."

"Which was?"

"He believed the president, in going into Iraq and Afghanistan, and in killing people with drones, had acted far outside his Constitutional powers. He believed the government had been betrayed by two administrations. This made him susceptible to the suggestion that other governments wouldn't dream of warmongering. Such as China, for example. Turns out he had minored in Asian History in college. He loved Asia and was extremely knowledgeable. The next step was not that far from the others."

"Which was?"

"Suggesting he should help an Asian country prepare to defend itself from the coming U.S. incursion. He really believed--maybe still does--the U.S. has its sights next set on China. That the U.S. will find some rationale to invade there before twenty-twenty-five."

"Why would the U.S. do that? Why would he even think that?"

"Simple. The United States' future is mortgaged to the Chinese. They hold almost twenty trillion in U.S. tax dollars that haven't even been collected yet. The national debt is horrifying to many Americans, counselor. Especially conservatives."

"So he agreed to sell national secrets?"

"He agreed to procure and sell U.S. war game planning. The Chinese are strategizing in response to U.S. invasion strategies of the Chinese mainland. The U.S. plays war games all day long against everyone. Especially the Asians. As economies change, as the weather kills off certain crops and tsunamis annihilate coastal populations, so do U.S. needs and interests change along with them. So the war games are constantly in flux. Our friends in China pay top dollars for the latest iteration. With this information they strategize their responses. It's all gamesmanship, counsel, and your client accepted millions of dollars for selling these games to the Chinese. Did I answer that?"

"You did. War games for money. Except?"

"Except the games we provided him to sell weren't real. They were skewed as far from reality as we thought we could skew them without anyone catching on."

"And where did the war games come from? Surely a U.S. Attorney wouldn't have access to them."

"No, but a certain worker in the Department of Defense did. A low-level computer scientist against whom the U.S. Attorney's office had threatened prosecution. Broyles threatened the man and the man coughed up disinformation. We were there pulling strings every step of the way. Brilliant, yes?"

"It's brilliant thus far, nobody disputes that. But what if Broyles testifies that he knew all this and that he was in on it, that he was actually a double agent?"

"I moved him from a conversation with me to a conversation with real Chinese spies. This was done in a manner I cannot disclose. But make no mistake. Your client believed he was a traitor. Everything he did points to that, from how he slunk around and covered his tracks to how he used satellite phones to make his calls. It was all very hush-hush and he played like only a real spy would."

"Agent Chin, my client's movements and behaviors could just as well have been those of the double agent, am I correct?"

"If you mean would a double agent do certain things to make it look like he was a real traitor, then yes, I have to give you that."

"Thank you. So, we are left with your word and the word of Agent Ranski as the only proof my client was a traitor, isn't that the bottom-line?"

"That, and his threats against the DoD employee."

"Will he or she be called to testify?"

"National security forbids that. It will not happen."

"So my point is well taken. This case you've brought against Frank Broyles directly rests on the testimony and claims of you and Agent Ranski, correct?"

"I suppose so."

"And if the jury disregards your testimony or finds it suspect or just doesn't believe it, then this case against Frank Broyles must fail, correct?"

"Yes. Correct. With one minor reservation, of course."

Thaddeus paused. His eyes bored into the witness. He decided to take the chance. He was about to learn about asking open-ended questions where the answers weren't known beforehand.

"What would that reservation be, Agent Chin?"

"You yourself witnessed Franklin J. Broyles passing secrets to the Chinese. You witnessed it and you said nothing about it."

A flash of revelation exploded in Thaddeus' mind. So that was it! They were going to include him in Broyles' undercover scheme. He tried to think through this new miasma but his thoughts were scattered and fraught with enough threads to lead nowhere all at once if he paused to think them through. Not only that; there was seriously no time to reflect. The jury was waiting for him to contradict what had just been said about keeping quiet in the face of traitorous acts.

Which contradiction never came.

"I was instructed by Assistant U.S. Attorney Melissa McGrant and FBI Special Agent Naomi Ranski to follow Frank Broyles one night, it's true. But did they advise you that I was told to do these things in defense of the homeland? Did they advise you that I was told to do these things to help nail a traitor?"

"Objection!" cried the U.S. Attorney, Ollie Anderson. "Sidebar, please, Your Honor."

Judge Barnaby curled his index fingers at each attorney. "Come," he said simply. They joined him at sidebar. The U.S. Attorney went first.

"Judge," he whispered, "counsel is evidently a witness in this case. It is unethical for an attorney to also be a witness in his client's case. The government asks for Mr. Murfee's immediate disqualification as attorney of record in this case."

The judge looked down his long nose at Thaddeus. "Well?"

Thaddeus was still shaken. How the hell could this have escaped him? He was, in fact, a witness. It had just never occurred to him what that meant in the real world of trials and judges. Until then.

"Judge, it's true, I was instructed by my supervisor Melissa McGrant to follow Frank Broyles. And I did that. But the witness has said that was a traitorous act and he has testified about it. I have not been listed on the government's list of witnesses as a witness having knowledge of those things. So I did not consider myself a witness."

"That's flaming bullshit, counsel," hissed the judge. "And you know it. You have committed a serious ethical violation here and I intend to report you to the bar and have your license to practice law revoked. I am also open to holding you in contempt of my court, but I'll reserve making that holding until morning. I don't want it said that I threw your ass in jail while I was angry. I'll wait until my anger has passed and then throw your ass in jail for a long time. But in the meantime, your client's interests are paramount here. We are continuing this trial. The attorney is not removed as counsel but he is certainly censured by the court. Return to your places, gentlemen, I have a trial to run."

Thaddeus and the Assistant U.S. Attorney returned to their tables. Thaddeus leaned to Matheson and whispered something to him, something like, "Smile so the jury knows we're taking this lightly right now."

Matheson did as he was told. He smiled. Thaddeus did as well. Meanwhile, Judge Barnaby was staring daggers at them, his rage barely concealed behind his stormy demeanor and pursed lips.

Then Thaddeus took up where he had left off. It was time to close down the cross-examination and get the hell out of Dodge, he would later tell Nikki.

"Thank you, Agent Chin. I have nothing further, Your Honor."

Judge Barnaby looked up at the wall clock. Just before noon. He called a recess and nodded at the marshals. Thaddeus was again taken into custody, this time to spend his lunch hour incarcerated in the court's holding cell. Matheson promised to return with sandwiches and a thermos of coffee and the marshals made no objection.

Thaddeus was left sitting offstage in the holding cell, alone.

He opened his laptop and went to work.

26

After lunch hour, Thaddeus was moved by the marshals from the holding cell back into the courtroom. He took the remaining fifteen minutes before court started back up to confer with Matheson and Broyles. Both men agreed that the government would probably rest. A call was placed to Melissa McGrant's office to advise her she would be needed pursuant to subpoena as soon as court took up again.

Sure enough, after getting underway, the government abruptly announced that it was resting its case. All eyes turned to Thaddeus. It was time for the defense to have its say.

"Defense calls Melissa McGrant," Thaddeus boomed loud enough for the bailiff to hear so that he could go outside the courtroom and retrieve McGrant to testify. Which he did. Just minutes later she was being sworn and took a seat in the witness chair. Her perfect bow of a mouth appeared stress-free and her violet eyes flashed friendly at the jury.

She was ready and Thaddeus inwardly flinched at her cool calm. This was going to be an uphill battle.

"State your name."

"Melissa McGrant."

"What is your business, occupation, or profession?"

"I am an attorney with the United States Department of Justice, permanently assigned to the Office of the United States Attorney."

"What is your job title?'

"Trial Attorney One."

"What are your duties?"

"I head up a team of trial lawyers."

"What kind of cases does your team handle?"

"Right now? Espionage."

"Would that include the case that we're here about today?"

"Yes it would."

"Why aren't you trying this case?"

She smiled and looked over at the jury. She cooed, "Like you, counsel, I too am a witness in this case. However, unlike you, I have determined that fact disqualifies me from acting as trial counsel in the case. I believe it would be unethical for me to try the case. Evidently you believe otherwise."

He turned very red above his white collar. She had nailed him fair and square. Point taken, time to move along.

Deciding to jump right at her, he wasted no time with further preliminaries.

"Attorney McGrant, isn't it true that you solicited me to make undercover sales to the Chinese for you?"

"Objection!" cried the U.S. Attorney. "Sidebar, please."

The judge again motioned both attorneys up to his perch.

"Judge," Ollie Anderson sputtered, "this subject is a matter of vital national security. Whether Mr. Murfee was solicited to work undercover against the Chinese is a matter that pertains to vital national interests. I would have thought Mr. Murfee would have the commonsense to avoid this altogether!"

"Mr. Murfee?"

"Judge, national security claims are an attempt to silence me. The fact the United States solicits people to work undercover is the stuff of nightly TV drama. It has no place in a federal courtroom as an element to muzzle the defense in a case of this importance. This is a capital case, Your Honor. My client could be sentenced to death if convicted of the charges against him. I strongly oppose being muzzled and told I can't bring to the jury's attention compelling testimony about what actually happened here."

Judge Barnaby, to Thaddeus' surprise, didn't look askance at him this time. Nor did he threaten him with incarceration. Instead he said, simply, "The objection is overruled. Counsel you may inquire into this area. Just be damn sure it doesn't leak over into unrelated matters that involve national security. You could spend another night or two in jail if that were to happen."

The attorneys returned to their places and Thaddeus again faced the witness. The judge overruled the objection on the record.

"Well?" Thaddeus said to the witness, "isn't it true you solicited me to make undercover sales to the Chinese for you?"

McGrant slowly shook her head. Later, upon reflection, Thaddeus would wonder whether she actually was feeling sorry for him at that point. Because he was about to make himself a clear and undeniable witness in his own client's case. Luckily, Matheson piped up.

"Your Honor," said Matheson before McGrant could reply, "may I have five minutes with Mr. Murfee? An issue has come to my attention and we need to talk."

"We're in recess fifteen minutes," said the judge.

"All rise," cried the bailiff and the courtroom stood and stretched while Matheson led Thaddeus out into the hallway by the arm.

Matheson's face was red and looked capillary-charged as he all but shouted, "What the hell are you doing, Thad? You're about to make yourself a clear and necessary witness in your own client's trial when she answers and denies that she ever solicited you to sell to the Chinese. If she gets to say that, you are left in a position where you yourself have to take the witness stand and tell all about what she did with you. You don't want that, son. You don't want to be a witness in your man's case. So far it's not looking all that bad for your guy--it's two FBI agents' word against Mr. Broyles' word. That is pretty flimsy. Go with that and you just might save his ass. But go down this road and take the witness stand and you're cluster-fucked, friend. You'll never come back from where the U.S. Attorney will take you on cross-examination. You will virtually ensure your client goes to jail, or worse. Now get back in there and withdraw that question. Then you can go into her dealings with Broyles, but stay far away from her dealings with you. *Capisce*?"

"Understand. Okay. Thanks."

Ten minutes later, when court resumed, Thaddeus withdrew the question. He then tacked downwind.

"Ms. McGrant, you had a special relationship with Mr. Broyles, did you not?"

"I wouldn't call it special. He was the head of the office where I worked. But I was autonomous."

"He didn't interfere with your prosecution of espionage cases?"

"No, he didn't."

"And he didn't interfere with your investigation of espionage cases?"

"Not really. Especially not when he was the subject of the investigation. I was brought in on that by the FBI at the front end."

"How could you keep quiet, knowing that your boss was selling top secret information to the Chinese?"

"Aha! Not so! It was all disinformation, so I was very warm to it, once I understood he was betraying his own country. Then I wanted nothing but to catch him and prosecute him."

"Yes, about that. What proof do you have of what you just said? That he was selling secrets to the Chinese?"

"Hours--days and days--of surveillance video, photographs, and telephone conversations. That's what I have."

"All right, and what proof do you have that he wasn't cooperating with you, your prosecution arm, and was in fact acting as a double agent?"

"Double agent? You mean working for the government while appearing to be involved in espionage against his government?"

"That's what I mean. How can you prove he wasn't doing whatever he was doing with the full advice and consent of the government?"

"My word against his. Agent Ranski's word against his. Agent Chin's word against his."

"But no documentary proof? No surveillance proving he wasn't working for you? Nothing written or recorded to prove he wasn't working for you?"

"Of course not. We would never keep proof of that. It could too easily fall into the wrong hands."

"All right. Now tell the jury how they're supposed to vote guilty when you haven't proven this case beyond a reasonable doubt? Look over there and tell them."

She did as requested, looking at the jury with a professional smile and nod.

"Ladies and gentlemen, you have the word of three officers--two of them FBI and one of them DOJ--that the defendant in this criminal case was, in fact, a criminal acting alone when he sold secrets to the Chinese. That is enough to convict him and I hope you do just that. Thank you, Mr. Murfee, for this chance to speak directly to the jury."

He kicked himself. He would sure as hell never do that again.

Thaddeus stumbled around a few more minutes with the witness then decided to let the patient expire. There was nothing useful to gain at that point and she was only improving in the quality of further answers to his follow-up questions.

Cross-examination was brief and only rehashed how compelling the case was against Broyles. In the end, Thaddeus was wishing he'd never called McGrant to the witness stand. Now he had hurt his defense case and was looking rather amateurish.

27

They needed the Chinese man. So they sent Matheson's investigator along with Thaddeus to find him. The plan was to locate the guy and serve him with a subpoena. If he failed to appear in court the judge would issue a bench warrant and he would be dragged into court. Then the jury would get to see the enemy up close and that would take the focus off Broyles. Moreover, Thaddeus could ask him whether he knew Broyles. He wanted the guy in court badly.

Rick Morrissey was a young private investigator who had started out in the Sheriff's office, lost his hearing in one ear when a suspect's kitchen stove exploded, and wound up earning a PI license. He had been picked up by Matheson and made his full-time investigator. As far as Matheson was concerned the guy was worth his weight in gold.

Thaddeus asked the judge for a conference in chambers when the trial ended for the day. Judge Barnaby rolled his eyes and summarily denied the request, but had second thoughts and wearily ushered the trial lawyers into his office. Defendant Broyles was brought along, too, as well as the court reporter and two marshals to escort Thaddeus and Broyles back to jail when the hearing ended.

Judge Barnaby pulled a Heineken out of his mini fridge, unscrewed the cap and tossed it into the wastebasket. He offered a drink to no one else, instead unzipping his robe with his back to his audience as he gulped down his first drink of the day. Only then did Thaddeus put two and two together. The man's rage was the rage of the alcoholic. He knew it all too well, for he still remembered his mother's eyes and voice--and rage--from long, long ago. Now he wondered how he had missed it all along. He had been treating Barnaby as a rational man when the guy was anything but. The whole trial suddenly fell into focus for him and, for the first time since starting law school three years ago, he began seeing the possessors of the law--the professors and now the judges--as human beings with frailties and foibles galore to whom he had ascribed far deeper thoughts than what they actually had between the ears. They were men just like him. No more, no less, and certainly no more knowledgeable. He had no doubt that hereafter he would be able to not only keep up with them but even to surpass them when it came to the game of law. He was catching on.

At last the judge sat behind his desk, pushed back--presumably not to breathe on anyone--and looked impassively at Thaddeus.

"Mr. Murfee? You have something to say to the court?"

Thaddeus fought down the urge to stand. Standing while addressing the court was the norm; the informality of a judge's chambers was still lost on him. He looked directly at

Judge Barnaby, refusing to flinch even when the pained voice of the bedeviled was aimed at him.

"Yes, Judge, I have something to say. For the record, this court has sentenced me to yet another night in jail. Rightly or wrongly done, I will gladly serve the time. However, the court's timing is the worst possible, because tonight I have an errand to run that only I can run. The errand is directly related to my preparation of my client's defense. For the court to deny me the opportunity to run this errand and thus prepare my client's case is prejudicial and cries out for reversal on appeal."

"What errand might that be, Mr. Murfee?" the judge asked, stifling a yawn.

"Please don't make me say, Your Honor," Thaddeus replied. "It would degrade my client's case in chief to have to disclose his strategy at this moment."

"Please, Mr. Murfee, how am I to rule if I don't know what I'm ruling on? Even you can understand that, correct?"

Even you--it echoed in his mind several times, the blame and shame that always came with to quench his spirit when it was said. But then he literally grabbed himself by the scruff of his neck and stood up on his legs and struck back, sending the shame right back at the giver.

"Judge, that's easy for you to say. You've already chugged down a whole beer and are feeling no pain. It's easy for you to toy with me and emasculate my defense. People like you are filling up the barrooms right now at five o'clock as we speak. All getting ready to lie to each other, hit on each other, and cheat each other. You fall somewhere in there, telling me that even I can understand your thought process. I can assure you, sir, that Sigmund Freud himself would find it difficult to unravel your thoughts. I certainly can't, so please don't try to hang it around my neck."

Barnaby almost fell over backwards in his chair. Leaning back as he listened, Thaddeus' words jolted him upright and made him reach and grab the edge of the desk to right himself.

"Mr. Murfee!" the judge cried, obviously stunned. "Never in twenty-two years have I been talked to like that!"

Said Thaddeus, "I can assure you it's not because you didn't deserve it somewhere along the way."

"You, sir, will spend the next thirty days in jail. We are on the record and your contempt of the court is clear."

"That's all well and good, but what about my errand tonight? Will the court allow me to at least prepare the defense of my client's case? Does death by lethal injection compel you? Or does that hurt the court's feelings so much that my client's constitutional rights are kicked to the side of the street by Your Honor?"

The judge looked at Matheson and winced. "You should remove your co-counsel, Mr. Matheson. Please do. Mr. Murfee, your jail time begins tomorrow at noon break and every recess thereafter. But tonight, you're free to prepare your client's defense, and God help him. Following the verdict in this case you will be returned to jail for thirty days. That is all, gentlemen and Mr. Murfee."

"Thank you, Judge," said Matheson. He had taken hold of Thaddeus' arm and was pulling him upright.

"Thank you, Judge," said Thaddeus. "It's the right thing, what you're doing."

"Court is adjourned until morning."

Matheson and Thaddeus followed the other attorneys and marshals outside into the hallway.

"Bastard," Thaddeus hissed at Matheson. "He's a low-life bastard, that man."

"Get hold of yourself, Thaddeus. It's over; you won. Now let's find my investigator and get going on this."

They found investigator Rick Morrissey reading *People* in Matheson's waiting room on LaSalle Street. The youthful investigator scrambled to his feet and extended his hand to Thaddeus. Introductions were made and Thaddeus asked Morrissey if he were ready. Morrissey only smiled. "Who's driving?" he asked. Thaddeus said that he owned only a motor scooter so they took Morrissey's Pathfinder.

Thaddeus gave directions to the house in Virginia where he'd last seen the man who'd met Broyles at the reservoir. Travel time was almost an hour, given the stop and go rush hour traffic and given that they got lost several times on the way. At last, however, they pulled up at the long circular driveway and the SUV stopped. Morrissey looked across at Thaddeus.

"Now what?" he asked.

"Now we wait and see who's coming and going. Until the right guy shows up."

"If he's going to show up at all. I don't like your plan, counselor. I suggest we march up to the front door, flash our fake badges, and announce that we're from the sheriff's office and we've received a complaint."

"A complaint of what?"

Morrissey smiled. "Let me take care of that. Here, take this."

He rummaged around in the console and produced several gold badges clipped inside leather wallets, police detective style. Thaddeus chose one and put it in an inside coat pocket. Morrissey did likewise. Then off they went, pulling up the driveway and parking at the entrance to the house.

It was set back, so they walked along the sidewalk. Thaddeus felt his pulse quicken as the moment of truth approached.

Morrissey rang the doorbell. After a full minute and no answer, he rang again. Footsteps could be heard inside.

The door opened, and there stood a withered old Chinese gentleman wearing a smoking jacket, a *Post* pinched between his thumb and finger. Reading glasses were pushed up on his forehead. He looked like a wispy old owl, comfortable enough, and harmless, thought Thaddeus.

Morrissey produced his badge and flashed it at the man.

"Sir, we're with the sheriff's department. May we come in?"

Without a word the old man stood aside and allowed entrance. He neither spoke nor changed expression. It was all in a day's work, his impassive face said.

"May we sit here in the family room?"

"Please do," said their host recruit.

They took chairs in the carpeted family room as the old

man muted the blaring TV that had greeted them. Then he turned and swung his chair around to face them. His light brown eyes looked them over in turn as he waited for someone to tell him what was up.

Morrissey went first.

"We're with the sheriff's department and we have reason to believe there is someone living here who is in danger."

"Danger? What kind of danger?"

"A threat has been received by us. Could you tell us who else lives here?"

"Who are you with?"

"The sheriff's department. We're investigators for the department. I'm Rick Morrissey. James Grand is my partner."

Thaddeus nodded. He would play James Grand if that was what it was going to take. For that matter, he would play just about anybody, though he wondered whether they had done the right thing by barging in. Wouldn't they have done better by hiding and waiting to see if the right man was spotted coming or going? He had never played cops and robbers in real life, so he didn't know. All he could do was follow Morrissey's lead.

"We're police officers," Thaddeus volunteered, entering into the game. "We're looking for someone who might be in serious trouble."

"Oh. Well, several people live here. We're all distantly related."

"Could we speak with the others?" Morrissey asked.

"You could, but no one else is here just now."

'They'll be returning when?"

"Around six or seven o'clock. Something like that."

"Does one of them work in downtown Washington?" Thaddeus asked on a thin hope.

"My grandson. He works in the embassy. The Chinese Embassy."

"That would be on International Place?"

"That's the one," said the old man. "My name is Zhu. He's my grandson and I'm very proud."

"Good for you," said Morrissey. "Is there some way you can call him and ask him to hurry on home? We don't have much time."

"We can't stay long," Thaddeus added. He eyed the shoulder bag in Morrissey's lap. Contained within was the subpoena they hoped to serve. If only the chance arose. It could save Broyles' life, Thaddeus believed, though he wasn't sure just how that would happen.

"I can try his cell," said their host. He pulled a phone from his breast pocket and punched a button.

A flurry of Chinese erupted once the call was answered. Whoever was on the other end could be heard spitting out rapid-fire sentences back at the old man. For his part, the man got to say very little. It came mostly from the other end.

The call concluded.

"He said to tell you he's in trouble and you are to leave at once. So please, go now."

Morrissey didn't miss a beat.

"Can't do that, sir. This is official police business. Lives are at stake. We must see this through."

"Oh," said the old man. "Then would you please wait outside in your car? Sing Di doesn't want you here."

"What's his name?"

"Sing Di Hoa. My grandson. Please go to your car, please."

"No can do," said Morrissey. Thaddeus had been ready to get up and go, but he relaxed when the investigator replied to the old man. The fact of the matter was that the old man really couldn't force them to leave. He could always call the cops but that wouldn't occur to him because he clearly believed they were cops. It was a stalemate.

"I can offer tea, if you insist on staying. But that is all."

"Tea would be most welcome," Morrissey replied. "Thank you."

A half hour later, a red sedan pulled into the long driveway and parked directly out front. Thaddeus, peering out through the front blinds, recognized the man--he thought. It looked like that the man he had followed home from the reservoir, the same man he met at the Washington Monument, but he wasn't certain.

As he came through the front door and found Morrissey blocking his way, the man looked directly at Thaddeus.

"That's him," Thaddeus said to Morrissey, who immediately handed the new arrival a sheaf of stapled papers.

"You've been served," Morrissey growled at the man. "Be in

court in the morning or the marshals will come for you. Don't try to flee the country; marshals have been notified you might try. You won't be allowed to leave."

"What is this about?" Hoa demanded to know.

"Frank Broyles," Thaddeus told him.

"Who?"

"Frank Broyles. You've been giving him money in exchange for U.S. secrets. Tomorrow morning you will testify about all that."

"I don't know what you're speaking of," Hoa said. "Please leave now."

"We're on our way out," Morrissey said. "Come along, Thaddeus."

"Thaddeus?" said the old man. "Who's Thaddeus?"

28

He didn't appear voluntarily. Thaddeus and Matheson had guessed that would be the case, so they called upon the Marshal's Service to send armed men to guarantee his appearance, which they did. By ten o'clock he was rounded up and brought handcuffed into court. The marshals stood him up before Judge Barnaby and stepped back. The jury was in place; all attorneys and investigators were in place, and Judge Barnaby went on the record, asking the man's name. He said he was Sing Di Hoa. Had he been served with a subpoena? He said he didn't know, but handed the papers served on him up to the judge. The judge took a quick look and told the man to take the witness stand. The marshals were told to remove the handcuffs and the witness was sworn by the clerk.

"Mr. Murfee, your witness." said the judge.

Thaddeus stepped up the lectern, notes at the ready, and plunged ahead. He asked and got the witness's name, address, and age. English-speaking and understanding capability was established as well, for the man spoke

English haltingly and several times had to ask for even the simplest question to be repeated. Still, Thaddeus moved it along.

"Mr. Hoa, where are you employed?"

"Employ?"

"Where do you work?"

"I work at the Chinese Embassy in Washington."

"What is your job title?"

"Title?"

"What is your job called?"

"Computer engineer. Network security."

"So your educational background is in computer science?"

"Science?"

"Uh, did you study computers at university?"

"My Ph.D. is in systems engineering. From the University of Beijing."

"How long have you had this job?"

"I have worked United States six months."

"Six months? Where were you before that."

"Before United States I worked in Beijing. Systems engineer there."

"Mr. Hoa, please take a look at this man right here," Thaddeus requested, moving around behind Frank Broyles and placing his hands on the defendant's shoulders. "Do you know this man?"

"No."

"Have you spoken with him before?"

"No."

"Have you met with him before?"

"No."

"Do you recall meeting him at the Georgetown Reservoir?"

"When?"

"This year. Well, at any time."

"No."

"Have you ever been to the Georgetown Reservoir?"

"Never been."

"Isn't it a fact you paid Mr. Broyles money for a briefcase at the Georgetown Reservoir?"

"No."

Thaddeus shuffled his feet at the lectern. This was making a point, but what was it? Only that the guy might as well have been some stranger of the street who was English-challenged? So he moved on to where he really wanted to be.

"Mr. Hoa, have you seen me before?"

"At my grandfather's house I saw you."

"Any other time?"

"No."

"You don't recall coming to a restaurant where I was eating lunch?"

"No."

"Mr. Hoa, isn't it true that within the past several months you came up to me while I was eating lunch at a local restaurant and tried to solicit me to sell you national security secrets?"

"Solicit? No solicit."

"You never offered me money to sell secrets to you?"

"No."

Now Thaddeus was flummoxed. But it was to be expected; obviously the guy wasn't going to implicate himself. Then Thaddeus thought he might be able to use the man as a tool for a different purpose. So he jumped back into his questions.

"Do you recall anyone from the United States Department of Justice ever telling you that they had got me to agree to sell you secrets?"

"Objection! Leading." Ollie Anderson was on his feet.

"Mr. Hoa is an adverse witness, Your Honor," Thaddeus answered back. "Leading should be allowed."

"Overruled. But there will be limits, Mr. Murfee. Please don't bore your audience. Or me."

Thaddeus ignored the judge. Prejudicial, as usual, but more fodder for appeal if Broyles were convicted, so he let it go.

"One last question. Mr. Hoa, the indictment in this case said that my client Franklin J. Broyles committed acts of espionage and treason by transmitting top secret documents to one Sing Di Hoa. That is your name?"

"Yes."

"Well, did Mr. Broyles ever transmit government secrets to you?'

"Never."

"Or to the Chinese Embassy in Washington?"

"Never."

"Or to any other Chinese person or entity?"

"Never."

"Thank you, Mr. Hoa. That is all, Your Honor."

"Mr. Anderson, does the government have any cross-examination?"

Ollie Anderson stood and said, sweetly, "He hasn't proven any facts in dispute, Judge. I don't see why the government would want to take up the court's time with cross-examination. We'll waive."

"Very well. Mr. Murfee, please call your next witness."

Thaddeus looked around the courtroom.

"Defense calls the records custodian for the U.S. Attorney's office, Washington, D.C."

All heads turned to look around.

When no one came forward, Thaddeus asked the court for a sidebar.

"Judge," he whispered when he and Anderson were gathered close to the bench, "I've subpoenaed the records custodian from the U.S. Attorney's office. Evidently he or she hasn't shown up yet. Can we recess until they show? I will notify Your Honor when they arrive."

Sick and tired of the animosity between himself and the young lawyer, Judge Barnaby agreed to recess. However--he counseled Thaddeus--they would resume no later than one hour from now. If Thaddeus had no further witnesses to call by then they would move to closing arguments and jury instructions.

Thaddeus went to the hallway at recess and called the U.S. Attorney's office. After being jacked around and switched off here and there, he at last was turned over to Melissa McGrant. She was the last person who'd had anything to do with Thaddeus. She was short and rude when he asked whether the records custodian was on the way to court.

"I don't know what you're talking about, Mr. Murfee," she said. "I haven't seen any *subpoena duces tecum* directed to any records custodian. I'm afraid you've got the wrong office. I'm hanging up now."

"No, no, no! I served the subpoena last week by mail."

"Mail isn't service. You need a marshal or process server to serve it on the U.S. Attorney or the manager of this office. Did you read the local rules? The *FRCP*? Do you even pay attention to the law, Mr. Murfee? Or are we all supposed to just jump in and help you out anytime you need it just because you're a nice guy. Well, you're not a nice guy and that will not be happening. Goodbye now, Mr. Murfee."

The phone line went dead.

Thaddeus checked his watch. Fifty minutes before trial was to resume. He leaned against the wall and closed his eyes. What to do?

Inspiration struck when he was considering how else he might obtain the files from Broyles' folder. He rushed down to the cafeteria and began typing furiously. When he was satisfied, he took his laptop upstairs and asked the clerk's office if they would allow him on the network to print his motion. After much hemming and hawing--but learning he was counsel of record of an ongoing trial--they agreed and the motion was printed. At the same time, it was filed with the court electronically. Thaddeus thanked the clerks who had pitched in. He ran back upstairs to Barnaby's courtroom. He re-read his work several times then went into the office of the judge's secretary. He handed her a courtesy copy of the motion for Judge Barnaby. She glanced it over and almost immediately began shaking her head.

"What?" he asked.

Her name was Linda and she controlled the office with an iron hand.

"Judge isn't going to grant this. You're asking the court to give you access to the U.S. Attorney's network. Judge Barnaby would never do that, Mr. Murfee. You need to do better than this."

A half hour later, the motion was heard in Judge Barnaby's chambers. Anderson, Thaddeus, and Matheson attended, along with the judge and his clerk. The court reporter rolled new paper into her machine and made ready.

Judge Barnaby slowly read the motion. He began shaking his head not ten lines into it. He scanned over the remaining two pages.

"The Court cannot do this, Mr. Murfee," said the judge. "It would jeopardize the government's entire computer system."

"What can I do to get at those files, Your Honor?" Thaddeus asked. "I sent a subpoena to the U.S. Attorney's records custodian but Ms. McGrant now tells me the service was improper. I--"

"Hold it right there, Mr. Murfee. The court is getting the feeling that we've come to a place in your inexperience where you're now asking the court to sweep up after you. You're asking me to clean up the mess you made by your inadequate service of process. I cannot and will not do that for you, Mr. Murfee. The subpoena and the necessary documents--those are issues that should have been worked out long before trial began. For the life of me I cannot begin to imagine how you could come to try this case without first acquiring these documents anyway, given what you say there are in this motion. They were far too important to put off until the last day of the defendant's case. Very poor work, sir. So the motion is denied. We'll go back in the courtroom and begin jury instructions now, gentlemen, unless Mr. Murfee has any other evidence or witnesses we need to hear."

"I don't have any other witnesses. And the evidence I need is on the new U.S. Attorney's file server. It's that simple."

"Can't help you there, Mr. Murfee," the judge said with a hint of glee creeping into his voice. "We stand in recess."

The court reporter sat upright and began scanning back over her tape. However, before anyone could leave, Thaddeus spoke up, angrily this time.

"Judge, my client's very life depends on me doing this case correctly. So far I've made lots of mistakes. But we've been able to clean those up, Mr. Matheson and I. This latest problem is definitely my fault too, but I'm begging the court not to hold it against my client Frank Broyles. He didn't create this situation and he was probably wrong in hiring me to defend him. But his error in judgment shouldn't get him executed or imprisoned for life."

"And?"

"So I would ask the court to continue the trial until tomorrow morning. Just give me that much time to figure out how to get the documents I need. Maybe there's another way and I'm missing it."

"Your Honor," Matheson said, leaning forward in his chair and speaking to the judge as if to an old friend, "Mr. Murfee is correct. It would be inappropriate and maybe require reversal on appeal for the court not to grant this brief continuance so Mr. Murfee can lay hands on the files he needs. If this case does require an appeal, I will be pursuing that. I'm confident I can not only get you overturned on this one issue alone, but I'm also confident I can talk the Court of Appeals into censuring you for not making this simple accommodation. I would urge the court to use its best judgment right now."

Judge Barnaby put his hands together and squeezed.

"My thoughts exactly, Mr. Matheson," Barnaby suddenly said, seizing on the warning he'd just been given. "Trial is recessed until eight o'clock tomorrow morning. Anything further?"

Thaddeus shot a look at Matheson. "Thank you," he mouthed. Matheson looked away.

"Then get out of here and let me get some work done. You gentlemen are dismissed."

Thaddeus headed for the door.

"Mr. Murfee," the judge called to him before he could escape. "Lockup waived this afternoon, but expect to find yourself back in jail tomorrow after court concludes. Don't plan on going to the Bahamas after you win your case."

Thaddeus didn't bother to respond. The tone was insulting and the reference to a trial win was sarcastic.

Out the door he went, followed close behind by Matheson and Ollie Anderson.

Once outside, Thaddeus spun around and faced Anderson head-on.

"Ollie, I need those records."

Ollie looked puzzled. "What is it exactly you're after?"

"Frank Broyles' files off the U.S. Attorney's server."

Ollie bit his lower lip. He checked his wristwatch.

"I'll see what I can do," he said softly.

Thaddeus wanted to hug the man, but restrained himself.

"Oh, my God, thank you," he said. "You don't know how much--"

Ollie spun around just as he was leaving.

"Thaddeus, I do too know. We were all idiots once. Right, Matt?"

Matheson could only nod.

"Were we ever," he finally managed. "And I was the biggest idiot of them all."

Ollie smiled. "You said it, not me."

29

Matheson had made an empty office available for Thaddeus' use once he was onboard. Thaddeus furnished it with a second-hand card table and three second-hand chairs that were unrelated to each other. In short, it was a mishmash.

Three hours into the afternoon Thaddeus was panicking. A solution to acquiring the Broyles files hadn't announced itself to him. And it was getting dusky outside. Offices all over D.C. would be closing for the day in less than one hour, including the office of the U.S. Attorney. Beads of sweat appeared on his forehead as he tried to force strategies onto the problem. Then he sat back and closed his eyes, imagining himself stealing into his old office at the U.S. Attorney's and making off with the files. But that wasn't going to happen, he realized with a start. Like Broyles, he no longer worked there. Like Broyles, he no longer had access to the network.

He was sitting at his table drumming his fingers on the flimsy top when Matheson's receptionist leaned in his door.

"Thaddeus. You have a visitor."

"Who?"

"Unknown. Young woman."

"Please show her in."

He'd seen her around the U.S. Attorney's office. She was generally in the company of a young male paralegal either coming from or going to lunch. They were inseparable and Thaddeus had once noticed how happy they appeared.

She came strolling in and took a seat across from Thaddeus without being asked.

"Ollie sent me. He says this meeting never took place. I'm to give you this. She opened her hand and there was a silver key. She moved her hand to the middle of the table and turned it over. The key fell to the quilted-vinyl table top.

"What is it to?" he wanted to know.

"Bus station. Locker number's on the key. Goodbye."

"Wait. Please, what is it?"

She shrugged. "Need to know. I'm not on that list."

"Well, thanks."

"One more thing, Mr. Murfee."

"What?"

"Ollie said to say, they are following you."

"Who is following me?"

"Sorry. Need to know."

"That's all he said about it?"

"Goodbye, Mr. Murfee."

"Goodbye. Please tell Ollie I said thanks."

"Tell who?"

He almost answered, then realized. This was the way it was done.

Thaddeus rode downstairs to the parking garage. His Vespa was parked in a slot that wasn't really a parking place but was a small island between the last car and the wall. Inserting the bike key, he fired it up and lifted his feet.

Up the ramp he rode, stopping at the pay arm to pass three dollars to the gatekeeper.

He played her words in his head: *Ollie said to say, they are following you.*

But who was "they?" Bottom line, it really didn't matter. He had the key and he was headed to the bus station and whoever might be following him was about to discover the real advantage of Vespa scooters. He ramped onto the freeway and joined stop-and-go traffic. With a simple turn of the handlebars he edged the bike into a position where he was suddenly moving forward between two lanes of stopped traffic. He turned the grip, accelerating even faster as he took a quick glance in the rearview mirror and confirmed: there was no one behind him on a similar rig. Which meant that whoever was following him had just been ditched. They sure as hell wouldn't be following him down this non-existent lane of traffic, he told himself. So that part was taken care of.

He came flying up New York Avenue and headed south to Union Station. Parking up next to the entrance in a designated motorcycle area, Thaddeus hurried inside the building. He pulled the silver key from his pocket and noted the locker number. 239E. By passing the 100's and making his way to the lockers in the 200's, Thaddeus became aware of a few men wearing black suits scattered through the milling crowd of people. It seemed--could it be?--they were watching him. But he decided that was paranoia and headed for 239. He realized, as he came upon a man with folded arms lingering at the 200 row of lockers, that it wasn't paranoia at all. The man looked him over and began coming up to him. Thaddeus abruptly spun on his heel and retraced his steps. He made it back outside the main doors, trying his best to melt away into the crowd of commuters leaving the building.

Then he was on his scooter and fleeing through the parking lot. Headlights bounced in behind him. He turned right at the row of parked cars and the headlights followed. He randomly turned left at the next row and sped up. The headlights did likewise, keeping tight on his trail. Then he realized. The headlights were close-set; in the early night light he looked again. It was a motorcycle and it was closing on him.

He panicked and made a run for it. Back out onto Massachusetts Avenue he blasted, giving his Vespa all the gas it would take. But it was useless. The motorcycle stayed right there. He ramped onto New Jersey Avenue and began filtering through the stop-and-go lines of traffic. The bike stayed right on him.

Pulling back into the underground parking at Mathewson's

building, Thaddeus saw the motorcycle break away, pull on up to the next corner, then sit off to the side, engine idling. It was the last he saw of his pursuer as he ducked underground and flew off to his parking slot beside the elevators. Back upstairs he went, closing his eyes and consciously trying to slow his racing heart. The office was locked but Matheson had kindly provided a key. Thaddeus let himself inside and went back into his office, where he flopped into his folding chair. A yellow message was centered on his desk. He picked it up.

Call Nikki. She's home.

Thaddeus couldn't punch her digits into his phone fast enough.

She picked up on the first buzz.

"Thaddeus!" she cried. "I had to come. I've withdrawn from school and I'm ready to help my dad's case. Just tell me what to do."

"Nikki, thank God you called. I really need your help with a project tonight."

"Just say when and where."

"Come to Matheson's building. Do you know where it is?"

She said she didn't; he gave instructions. She was to come to the building and meet him downstairs in the Oxbow Restaurant. She said to give her thirty and she'd be there.

He ended the call and sat back. Whoever was following--the FBI probably--was onto him, was onto Morrissey, and probably onto any and every one Thaddeus had involved in the case. But Nikki was an unknown. She had been away at school. He hoped upon hope: they would never see her coming.

Thirty minutes later, she walked into the Oxbow wearing jeans, a tan sweatshirt that said Redskins, and a black beret. No one came in after her. They hugged and she slid into the booth next to him.

"So," she said, turning to him, "how are we doing? Are we winning?"

He couldn't resist. For one, he was so glad to have someone step up to help him; but more than that, he was really glad to see Nikki. It had come to that, his thoughts of her, the pain of extricating himself from her life when it would have been wrong to stay entwined. Whatever; he was damn glad to see her. He leaned forward and met her lips with his. Neither made an effort to draw apart, even after several moments.

Then Thaddeus pulled back.

"First we have to save your dad. Then we'll talk. Here," he said, and he handed her the key from Ollie. "I need you to go to Union Station and bring back whatever's in this locker."

She took the key.

"Done," she said and, without another word, began sliding away. She stood up. "Don't leave here. I'll be back."

"Thank you, thank you, thank you," he said. "You're saving me."

She shook her head. "That's a nice thought, but I'm actually here to save my dad, Thaddeus."

"I know. Go!"

She was gone without his even having to say it.

He asked the waitress for a menu and started looking. There had been no food all day and he was famished.

FORTY-FIVE MINUTES LATER, Nikki returned. She pulled a long white envelope from beneath her sweatshirt and passed it across the table to Thaddeus. He slit it open with his dinner knife.

"Look," he said, and shook a flash drive out of the envelope. "This is all there was?"

She nodded. "All there was."

They made a dash for Thaddeus' office and his laptop.

At last--he was hoping. At last he might have a chance.

BY TELLING the marshals up front that she was his paralegal and he needed her along, Thaddeus was able to take Nikki inside the jail with him and meet with her father.

Frank Broyles was looking haggard and gaunt. Too many nights in jail without sleep and too many days without sunlight were taking their toll. Nikki cried out when she saw her father; tears rolled down her cheeks as she leaned into him and they hugged in the privacy of the attorney conference room. He patted her on the back and finally pulled away. "I stink," he told her.

Thaddeus flipped open his laptop, inserted the flash drive, and spun the machine around so Broyles had the keyboard.

"All right," Thaddeus told him. "I've looked it over. It appears we've been given your private folder from the U.S. Attorney's server."

"Oh my God!" Broyles exclaimed. "How did you--"

"Don't worry about it. The point is, you've been given a chance. Now tell me what we have here."

Broyles busied himself at the keyboard, clicking and scrolling, reading and grimacing, reading and smiling, for a good five minutes. Finally, he looked up and spun the computer back around to Thaddeus.

"Make paper copies of everything. You're about to walk me out a free man."

"What is it, Dad?" Nikki asked.

He turned to her at his elbow. "It's my ticket out of here, Nik. It's all there."

30

Twelve hours later, Franklin J. Broyles was called at trial by Thaddeus. He stepped up to the witness stand, where the clerk administered the oath.

"Mr. Broyles," Thaddeus began, "tell the jury about your work history."

"Five years as U.S. Attorney for the District of Columbia. Six years prior I was a partner at Dunphy McKesson."

"What is Dunphy McKesson?"

"A D.C. law firm specializing in white collar crime."

"That was your area of expertise?"

"It was."

"And before that?"

"Before that I was a staff attorney at the Attorney General's office. I worked RICO cases that I'm not at liberty to discuss."

"Enough said. How long were you an Assistant U.S. Attorney?"

"Eleven years. That's been the majority of my career."

"So you've basically worked for the government your entire career."

"Except for the Dunphy years, that's right."

"And your practice area has been criminal law?"

"Yes. There was some civil law early on, some RICO seizure work, but that was too long ago for me to remember much."

"Mr. Broyles, when I gave my opening statement to the jury, I promised I would prove to them the true nature of your work in the U.S. Attorney's office. Do you remember me making that promise?"

"I do."

"I'm going to ask you now to help me keep that promise. First off, havé you ever worked for the government in any other capacity than as a lawyer?"

"Yes, I have."

"Please describe that."

Broyles sat back in the witness chair and tugged at his tie. Then he turned and faced the jury head-on.

"I worked for the government as a double agent."

"What does that mean?"

"I sold false information for the government to the Chinese."

"Why would you do that?"

"Because my government asked for my help and I agreed to help."

"But now you're here being prosecuted by that same government. How could that happen?"

"By a turn of fortune, I came into foreign banking records that proved some Washington lights were hiding money offshore."

"What's that mean, 'hiding money?'"

"Avoiding income taxes. What they do is get paid for this or that, usually by lobbyists. Except the payments go into a Hong Kong bank. The IRS doesn't get its cut."

"So you were prosecuted because of this?"

"Well, I would't turn over the records to my handlers."

"Why not?"

"Just in case the government ever came after me. I would have something to trade."

"Do you still have the records?"

"I do."

"What do you plan to do with them?"

"Take them to the *Washington Post* once this is all over."

"So your theory is you're being prosecuted in anticipation of turning them over. They're smearing you."

"That, and plausible deniability."

"Tell us what you mean by that."

"Plausible deniability. Uncle Sam never acknowledges the spy who gets caught. Or the spy whose usefulness has expired. Which is what happened to me. The Chinese decided they would no longer deal with me. The government kicked me to the curb because I had records I wouldn't turn over. I was indicted for treason and espionage so it looked like I was operating on my own. It happens."

"It happens? The government discards those who've helped spy for it?"

Broyles smiled sadly. "Yes. That's what happened to me."

"Used up and discarded."

"Used up and discarded."

"Let's talk about proof of what you say. Can you prove that you were acting at the government's request?"

"Yes, I can. It's all right there in the papers you printed out last night."

Thaddeus raised his hand off the two-inch pile of paper he had taken with him to the lectern. Early that morning they had each one been marked as an exhibit in the clerk's office. Now they were ready to be admitted into evidence. For next three hours, then, Thaddeus and Broyles went through the pile exhibit-by-exhibit, admitting each and all of them into the defendant's case.

At several times, special note was taken of the documents. It happened early on the first time.

"I'm going to hand you what's been marked Defendant's Exhibit fifty-five. Can you tell us what that is?"

"That's an email I received from Melissa McGrant."

"That would be the same Melissa McGrant who testified here during the government's case against you?"

"Yes."

"Please read the email to the jury."

"'TO: FJB. FROM: MM.'"

"Now who are FJB and MM?"

"Franklin J. Broyles and Melissa McGrant."

"Please proceed."

"'Your first package will be found in locker 239E. Your meeting is tonight at eight. Georgetown Reservoir, sluice gate. The man you are meeting is Chinese. Do not speak to him. Turn over the documents. He will pay you fifty-thousand dollars. The minute he gives it to you, turn and walk away. Then drive back downtown, take the money to your office and put it inside your top right-hand desk drawer. Then go home. That is all. DE.'"

"What is DE?"

"Destroy Email. Everything was signed like that."

"Why would the government use email, which could be saved and traced?"

"It expedited things. If you checked closely you'd learn that the email is sent from servers that cannot be traced to the government. The government has thousands of people like me passing out phony documents. It's a huge operation and it's run by email and cell phones. I was just a cog among thousands of other cogs in a great big machine. I was basically a nobody to them. As you'll see."

The testimony then moved on from there.

"Mr. Broyles, have you heard the term 'handler' before?'

"I have."

"What's a handler?"

"That's the person who manages the field agent."

"Who was your handler?"

"I had two. Melissa McGrant and Naomi Ranski."

"We know Melissa McGrant, she testified. The Naomi Ranski you are referring to--she also testified here against you?"

"Yes, the same."

"So the government turned on you by using the two people who were closest to you?"

"Yes."

"How did that make you feel?"

"Scared witless. I had no one to stand up for me and tell the truth. Fortunately, I had saved all of this evidence you obtained for me."

"Even though you were told to destroy it?"

"Even though. I've been a lawyer a long time, Mr. Murfee, and I've seen how our government can behave when it gets caught with its pants down. I wasn't going to be part of that without some protection of my own. So I saved everything I could."

"Next up we have six photographs. Please explain."

"These were taken at a Georgetown restaurant. They show me having dinner with Melissa McGrant and Naomi Ranski."

"Who took these and why?"

Broyles smiled and nodded.

"Yes, I had these taken by a man I hired. I was documenting my meetings with my handlers. Just because I knew it could potentially reach the point where they denied ever meeting with me or handling me with the Chinese."

"But this is only a photograph with the two of them. What does it actually prove?"

"If you look here at the briefcase on the floor, it has my initials just below the handle, FJB."

"All right. So what?"

"In photograph--" he paused to scan the exhibit list and find what he was looking for--"two-oh-two, you will see me handing over this same bag to Mr. Hoa, who you called as a witness and who denied knowledge of me. He is receiving the same briefcase from me, complete with the same initials as the first photograph. Here it is, Defendant's Exhibit two-oh-two."

"Same guy taking the pictures?"

"Same guy."

"So these two photographs show you with your government handlers plus the briefcase that you next are seen handing over to Mr. Hoa. Same initials. Plus it contradicts Hoa's story that he doesn't know you, never met with you, and so on."

"Yes. Mr. Murfee, I've been around espionage cases as well as undercover surveillance for many years now. I knew the only way I could do this was to document my role and protect myself."

Thaddeus looked off to his right at the jury. Notes were being furiously scribbled even as he watched. Plus the documents were being passed to them by Homer Matheson. Many jurors were shaking their heads and making notes about exhibits passing in front of them. Thaddeus slowed his presentation in order to accommodate their multitasking.

They continued admitting exhibits into evidence and producing commentary that described and explained why the exhibits were relevant. Thaddeus noted--with no small gratitude--that during the entire day of testimony Ollie Anderson made no objections. He was content to sit back and allow Broyles to defend himself. Thaddeus would come to learn that it was Broyles who had hired Anderson in the first place, many years ago. He gave Ollie a chance to redeem himself after being let go from a D.C. criminal law firm that decided Ollie wasn't carrying his weight. Ollie would tell Broyles that his billings had fallen off by half after a jury trial of a white collar price-fixing case that had gone on for six months and resulted in an unexpected finding of guilt. The entire thing had all but trashed the prosecutor's career but Frank Broyles had stepped up and taken him on. Broyles was compelled to: he had personally prosecuted the case Ollie lost. He had found Ollie to be an honorable and tremendously talented trial lawyer and he wasn't about to turn him away when Ollie came knocking. He hired him on the spot. Ollie had never forgotten.

Toward the end of Broyles' testimony, Thaddeus asked him, "Mr. Broyles, how far up the food chain does your case go? We know that Melissa McGrant was your handler. Did it go above her? If you know?"

Broyles took his time. He looked over at the jury, considering. Then he said, "Judge, what I have to say next is secret government information. Could you clear the courtroom?"

Judge Barnaby didn't like it, but he complied. Grumbling and out and out complaints to the judge followed, but in the end it was just the litigants, their representatives, the judge and jury.

Thaddeus then asked again, "Did someone sign off on all this who was above Melissa McGrant?"

"The president himself signs off on counter-espionage. It is run by the FBI, which is an arm of the Department of Justice, which is administered at the highest level by the president himself. But all counter-espionage efforts are vetted by the president."

"Are you saying he signed off each time you passed along documents?"

"Not at all. I'm saying he signed off on my doing this in the beginning."

"So we could call the president as a witness and, if he were to testify at all, he would acknowledge that you were acting at the government's request."

"Don't even think it, Mr. Murfee!" Judge Barnaby suddenly boomed from on high. "You will not be subpoenaing the president to testify in my courtroom!"

Thaddeus looked over at the judge.

"My," the young lawyer said warmly, "we are getting to know each other here, aren't we?"

"Enough, Mr. Murfee. Please wrap it up."

"Judge, the defense calls the president of the United States as its next witness."

"Mr. Murfee!" the judge erupted, "that is not going to happen! Now move on."

"I'm done with this witness, but I'm putting the court on notice that I am calling the president. Mr. Matheson, please prepare the president's subpoena."

"Mr. Murfee, is that all?" asked Judge Barnaby, ignoring for the moment the rest of it.

"Yes."

"The bailiff will re-admit the spectators and press."

Thaddeus then said he was finished with the witness.

"Counsel," the judge said to Ollie Anderson, "you may cross-examine."

"Mr. Broyles," said Anderson, "have you told the whole truth here today?"

"I have."

"And if you were called into a criminal case based on what we've heard here today, would you be willing to testify against Melissa McGrant and Naomi Ranski and any other government agents involved in bringing this prosecution against you?"

"I would."

"Then in that case the government is going to dismiss this case against you. With prejudice. Your Honor, the government moves to dismiss. With prejudice."

Judge Barnaby was stunned, as were Thaddeus, Broyles, and Matheson. The jurors sat with mouths open, expressions of relief on the faces of some, expressions of dismay on the faces of those who came to render a verdict.

"Very well," the judge said at last, "this case is dismissed with prejudice, meaning these charges can never be brought again. Ladies and Gentlemen, the court thanks you for your service. You are discharged. Mr. Murfee, you are remanded to the custody of the U.S. Marshal's service. You will now begin serving-out your thirty days' contempt sentence. We are in recess."

The two marshals in the courtroom descended upon him, fighting through the handshakes and hugs from Frank and Jeannette Broyles, from Nikki, from Homer Matheson, and attempts by the TV cameras to catch the participants on video. Thaddeus appeared briefly on camera as the marshals stood patiently off to the side, allowing him his few moments of glory. Then they unceremoniously escorted him from the courtroom with Nikki bobbing along at his side, telling him what she had planned for the two of them once he was released.

Broyles himself caught up with Thaddeus in the building lobby before the trio left for jail.

"Thank you, Thaddeus," said the ex-U.S. Attorney. "You've given me back my life. I'll be filing a motion myself in your case before the day is over, asking the court to reconsider its contempt citation against you. My guess is you'll be out of jail before noon tomorrow. Just enough time for Judge Barnaby to cool down."

Thaddeus laughed. "You do that and I'll give you your fee back. I've got a new girlfriend to take to dinner!"

"We'll see you tomorrow. Your first dinner with your new girlfriend is on me, incidentally. I couldn't be happier than to see you two having a glorious night out."

"Thank you, Mr. Broyles," Thaddeus said, extending his hand.

Broyles took it up and they shook hands.

The promise had been kept.

Franklin J. Broyles had been proven not guilty, just as the young lawyer had promised the jury in the beginning.

31

Ollie Anderson paid a visit to Thaddeus that night, just after the jail served a dinner of fish sticks and rice. The prosecutor had changed from his customary pinstripes to khakis and a blue broadcloth shirt open at the neck. The shoes were cross-trainers and the Senators baseball cap looked well-worn. They met in a visitors' meeting area though there were no other inmates or visitors there. Evidently the new U.S. Attorney had some drag around the jail, it occurred to Thaddeus as he was led there.

"Thaddeus," Anderson began, "let me congratulate you if I haven't already. It was a match well-played."

"Thank you. But it wouldn't have happened without you turning over Frank's file to us."

"It had to be done."

"But why? Most prosecutors I've heard about would never do that."

"Most of those prosecutors have forgotten the most important part of their job is not to win. It's to see that justice is served. The man needed his file to prove his case. I wasn't about to prevent him. It was only fair, Thaddeus."

"Well, I'm in your debt."

"No, you're not. But that's not why I'm here. I want to offer you your old job back in the U.S. Attorney's office. You would be ramrodding Team A in Cybercrimes."

"Seriously? You'd take someone who just beat--and probably embarrassed--the U.S. Attorney's office? That's more than I ever even dreamed of."

"Will you come back?"

Thaddeus hesitated. Then, "No, I don't think so. No."

"Why not?"

"I'm going somewhere small. Somewhere I can give my lack of experience the opportunity to catch up with my trial record of one and oh."

Anderson smiled.

"Smart man. That's very wise, Thaddeus."

"Thank you."

"So where are you going?"

"You know what? I'm just going to get out a map of the United States, close my eyes, and drop a pin. Wherever it lands, that's where I'm going."

"Well, if you ever need a reference--anything--just call me, please, Thaddeus."

"Thank you."

Thaddeus requested library privileges that night. He was gratified when he learned his name had been drawn. He would receive a trip to the library.

First thing, he found a map of the United States in a discontinued set of encyclopedias. Then he lifted his hand and closed his eyes. He plunged his index finger blindly down onto the map and opened his eyes.

Orbit, Illinois, was at the tip of his finger.

Now where in the world is Orbit? he wondered.

And why on earth would anyone ever go there? It was dead in the heart of flyover country, the Midwest.

But...Orbit it was. He had tempted the fates with his eyes closed and the fates had spoken.

He moved over to a computer and went online.

For the next hour he devoured everything about Orbit that he could find--which was actually very little.

But it was enough. He was already mentally back in his room packing his things, mentally crossing off what went with him and what got tossed.

EPILOGUE

But he didn't get out of jail that second night, nor the third nor the fourth. No, he got out of jail the same day he went in.

It seemed that Judge Barnaby had been approached by Homer Matheson and Ollie Anderson within the hour following the sudden dismissal of the government's case. Both men were outspoken and both were more than just a little upset with the Judge. They wasted no time letting him know they were upset, and why. They recited chapter and verse of the history of the court's dealing with Thaddeus Murfee, who came before it for his first time ever in any court, trying to understand the etiquette and gamesmanship of being a courthouse lawyer, and, rather than giving him some slack, the judge had pounced all over him and sent him packing off to jail every time the kid overstepped the boundaries of what was normal.

Judge Barnaby was no fool. He knew both men had at one time held positions of honor in the Washington Bar. Both men were well-known to appellate judges and the bar examiners. Anderson even sat on a bar examiner board, participating in membership decisions. And, because of their status, Judge Barnaby also knew the two men would have strong opinions about judicial complaints and which judges should be on the receiving end of such horrible missives. So, when they pled for leniency for Thaddeus, the judge reversed himself. He withdrew the finding of contempt and ordered the young lawyer released from jail immediately. Which happened just after Thaddeus had chosen Orbit, Illinois as his new home.

He kept company with Nikki for the following seven months. They stayed in D.C. so that Thaddeus could testify in Ollie's prosecutions of Melissa McGrant and Naomi Ranski. John Henry Fitzhugh—Thaddeus' original lawyer—represented Thaddeus at those trials just to make sure the train stayed on the rails.

Thaddeus arrived in the Midwest in early September. The leaves were changing and fall festivals were ongoing throughout the county. Beauty pageants were being held as the crops were harvested and the starting eleven of the Orbit High School football team flexed its on-field muscle at the end of his first week in town.

For her part, Nikki went a different direction. Having seen how her father was treated by the law, Nikki gave up on any plans of attending law school. She just could no longer predict a fun and interesting career in an industry where the old ate its young. And each other.

As a sophomore at Harvard Nikki had taken an elective in theater set design. The class had swept her off her feet and she'd gone on to participate in seven different productions during her next three years, including three musical comedies where the sets flew off and on the stage in dizzying succession. Her senior year found her in charge of that year's *Cats* production, and she excelled. Ever the local theater's severest critic, the *Harvard Crimson* celebrated Nikki's work on the production.

So Nikki trundled off to Hollywood to give it a try. She wanted to do set design and if she could land a job doing anything remotely connected, she would be thrilled. They kissed goodbye, Thaddeus and Nikki, in Springfield, Illinois, as they caravanned westward from Washington. She was going further west yet; he was almost to his new home, another fifty miles, tops.

"I'll always remember our time," she told him.

Tears came to his eyes. "I'll ask you one last time. Please stay."

"I would but I can't have my career in Orbit," she whispered against his cheek.

"I know that. But I have to ask. Don't be surprised if I keep on asking."

She pulled away and returned to her Highlander. She rolled down her window.

"You've got my digits," she said. "Please use them."

"I will, I'll call."

"Remember, Thaddeus, we will never back down, never give up."

"Never," he said, and touched her window as she rolled it up. Then she drove away into the night.

He fought down the tears and got behind the wheel of his new Chevrolet pickup.

The GPS malfunctioned just as he was about to pull out of the gas station. He turned it off and turned it back on. He flicked it with his fingernail, but it was no use. It couldn't locate Orbit.

So Thaddeus went inside the QuickGas and asked the young man behind the counter.

"Can you tell me how to get to Orbit?"

The young man, without looking up from the customer's bag of groceries, laughed. He looked up and caught Thaddeus' eye. Then he stopped packing as the customer turned to him.

"You can't get there from here," the customer said with a grin.

"Come again?"

"Second star to the right," said the customer's daughter, "then straight on 'til morning."

"Follow us. We're headed there."

Thaddeus stuck out his hand. "Name's Thaddeus Murfee. Thanks for the help."

"Killen Erwin," said the customer.

"My lucky night."

"Is it? I'm the District Attorney."

"That's where I knew you from. I saw your picture online the other night. When I was in jail."

"In jail for what?"

"It's a long story, but I'm a new attorney coming to town."

"You must not be a very good one, Thaddeus, not if you've already been in jail. You better come by the office in the morning and let me buy you a cup. You can tell me all about it."

"I'd like that," Thaddeus said. "I'm brand new."

"My family owns the motel. You can stay there tonight."

"That sounds perfect."

"Okay, see you tomorrow."

"Straight on 'til morning," said the little girl.

"Second star to the right?"

The little girl laughed. "You know Peter Pan?"

Thaddeus put on his most supremely serious look.

"Little girl, I *am* Peter Pan."

THE END

ALSO BY JOHN ELLSWORTH

THADDEUS MURFEE SERIES

Thaddeus Murfee

The Defendants

Beyond a Reasonable Death

Attorney at Large

Chase, the Bad Baby

Defending Turquoise

The Mental Case

Unspeakable Prayers

The Girl Who Wrote The New York Times Bestseller

The Trial Lawyer (A Small Death)

The Near Death Experience

SISTERS IN LAW SERIES

Frat Party: Sisters In Law

Hellfire: Sisters In Law

MICHAEL GRESHAM SERIES

Lies She Never Told Me

The Lawyer

Secrets Girls Keep

The Law Partners

CARLOS THE ANT

SAKHAROV THE BEAR

ANNIE'S VERDICT

DEAD LAWYER ON AISLE 11

30 DAYS OF JUSTIS

PSYCHOLOGICAL THRILLERS

THE EMPTY PLACE AT THE TABLE

ABOUT THE AUTHOR

John Ellsworth practiced law while based in Chicago.

For thirty years John defended criminal clients across the United States. He has defended cases ranging from shoplifting to First Degree Murder to RICO to Tax Evasion, and has gone to jury trial on hundreds. His first book, *The Defendants*, was published in January, 2014. John is presently at work on his 24th thriller.

Reception to John's books has been phenomenal; more than 1,000,000 have been downloaded in 40 months. All are Amazon best-sellers. He is an Amazon All-Star every month and is a *USA Today* bestseller.

John Ellsworth lives in Arizona in the mountains and in California on the beach. He has three dogs that ignore him but worship his wife, and bark day and night until another home must be abandoned in yet another move.

johnellsworthbooks.com
johnellsworthbooks@gmail.com

Cover design by Steve Richer: sricher@sympatico.ca.

Published by Subjudica Press, San Diego.

First edition

Ellsworth, John. *A Young Lawyer's Story*. Subjudica House. Kindle Edition.

EMAIL SIGNUP

If you would like to be notified of new book publications, please sign up for my email list. You will receive news of new books, newsletters, and occasional drawings.

— John Ellsworth